WHAT PEOPLE DO FOR MONEY

A James Hickman Book

Bent Publishing
College Park, Ga.

ISBN#: 978-1-4243-2965-6
Library of Congress control number: 2007900054

Back Photo: Dennis Byron

Cover Design: James Hickman & Markstarr Multimedia

Printed in the United States of America
Published by
Bullet Entertainment Group
5441 Riverdale Rd. Suite 129
College Park, Ga 30349
www.Bentpublishing.com
Email: bulletent4000@yahoo.com

To order additional copies wholesale, please contact James Hickman at 404-246-6496 or bulletent4000@yahoo.com

All the while Magic felt empty. All the smiles and flirting she did on a regular basis never made her feel complete. she loved her job but knew in order to make ends meet she would have to bring her plan she plotted constantly in her mind so she could have enough money to pay for the lifestyle she wanted, and no man could give her enough to fill this empty void that filled her heart constantly, The only thing a man could do was help her carry out her plans bringing them to fruition. The music became like a drug. All the dancer's that danced on stage all went to the edge 10 in all. The DJ announced it was touchy feely night. This gave men the permission they needed to touch their favorite dancers on their secret places. The man that watched Magic like a hawk commanded her to come to him. Magic walked to the edge of the stage she then backed away not feeling this. This was it; she couldn't see herself letting all those strange men feel her like she was a piece steak on the chopping block. This was some new shit the club had just introduced as a promotional gimmick and Magic was dead set against it. Time had come to bring her plan to light; the rewards would be sweet once everything was complete. She bumped past all the other dancers running to the back of the club in a heated rage.

"Magic you need to get back out there. This is the money making point of the night. Why are you running back here, is there something you're not telling me?' Dino asks.

'I'm not letting those freaks touch me all over my body; that not why I'm gainfully employed here.' Magic said as she slipped her skin tight hip hugger jeans on revealing all her sexy tattoo's on her lower back.

'You're fired! I can't have you walking around here telling me what you're not going to do so pack your shit and get out.' Then Dino said as he held the door opened forcing Magic to leave. Magic did just that she loaded up her Audi TT a male customer had given her for turning him on in a most usual way at a bachelor party. She drove through the streets of ATL thinking of the starting point of her plan. She stopped her car at a location where the jewelry store she dreamt of hitting sat. She sat there gazing into the window at four a.m. in the morning until she gained enough courage to walk over looking at the prizes that lay inside it was like another dimension between her and the diamonds that laid inside. This window display was some of the most expensive diamonds she had ever seen in her whole twenty five years and they were all pink. The gate that surrounded the store was thick and the security system tight. Her eyes got big as quarters wishing she could melt through the glass as she seen the light shine inside the store of security cameras and the glare of light that came from beneath the office door.

"I got to have those," Magic thought to herself not caring what kind of cameras or security systems blocked her way. She was determined to reach out and grab her dream. She knew in order to do this it would take lots of planning and plotting. Life in the ghetto was getting extremely boring and harder by the minute she craved a higher lifestyle. It was the wee hours of the morning; Magic was the only person window shopping at this hour. she stood there bent over checking out the beautifully displayed window until one of Atlanta's police cars drove by in a slow mode, and as it approach, the officer shined his bright flash light on Magic's backside as she continued to drool over the display.

"Is everything alright ma'am?' The cop asked as he stepped halfway out his car he noticed Magic had on a sexy outfit and wondered why she was out window shopping this early in the morning, after all the streets of Georgia is dangerous after a certain hour.

"Hi officer... everything's fine.' Magic said to the cop as she slowly turned around sporting a pink babyphat outfit with her big thighs and stiletto pumps on she flashed her pearly whites as she threw the cop a pleasant smile.

"Are you shopping tonight?' The cop asks in a friendly tone.

"No sir, just looking at this beautiful display that caught my eye on the way home from work. I just stepped out my car to check it out.' Magic pointed to her Audi TT and the officer seen her taste was expensive and her beauty impeccable he just got back in his car and drove off cutting on his cherry top speeding though the streets to another scene.

Magic returned to her Audi TT to drive home to her tiny apartment in the ghetto of the ATL in Bank head. She was no stranger to this neighborhood the same shit happened on her block that happens on every block in ghettos all across The United States of America. Magic was use to hearing gun shots twenty four seven and hearing sirens all night and most of the time during the day. She had come to a point in life where this was not enough. She had to prove to all the world she could be the hi powered women she always wanted to be and her blood, sweat, and tears brought nothing with it but sorrow, hurt, and pain. She had the car now it was time to get the big banging house and the bank account to compliment her taste this would help her to graduate to another level beyond her present condition. As she pulled up to her curbside door she got out of the car still thinking of who she could get to help her pull her dream scam off. She would be calling this one the dream that was to come. All her past tricks she turned had been with the thuggish type and the archetype of the I want to be player characteristics. Life wasn't worth living if she didn't have a gangsta there by her side to share the loot of the spoils she planned on getting one way or the other. Magic opened the door of her tiny apartment as her cat ran greeting her at the door. She grabbed hold of it carrying Blossom over to the couch where she flopped down kicking off her stiletto pump propping her feet up on the coffee table trying to find a relaxed mode. She needed guidance in life. she sat there quietly listening to her inner voice telling her and showing her pictures of who to approach on the level she was about to sojourn. A picture of a guy she met at the club years ago and brought home to have sex with popped into her mind. She wrote his name on her list of prospects along with others and the job functions she would ask him to do. This was the only road she knew to take to get what her spoil nature would not allow and if it meant breaking the law to get it she was willing to take the chance. She figure who would suspect a sexy stripper like her. She could pass this off and get what she wanted beyond the rules of reason.

She picked up her phone to dial Douglas number. He was good with electronic and she needed him now more than ever, a young thug with this much talent. Magic was willing to teach him how to use his traits for her if not for his self. She knew she could get him to bend to her will for a price. Magic didn't care what time it was, she called Douglas.

'Hello.' Magic said in a soft sexy voice using her karma sutra to turn him on at this most important and desperate moment in her life.

'Who in the hell is this calling me this early in the morning?' Douglas asks not feeling her vibes.

'Oh...it's like that now after you told me I could call you anytime.' Magic asks dumbfounded by his response to her sexy hello instead all was reversed.

'Magic, this you baby?' Douglas asked as he propped himself up in his bed surrounded with dirty clothes grabbing hold of the alarm clock that sat beside his bed on top of a mountain of Chinese food cartons and dirty laundry, boots and sneakers.

'The one and only and I need you Douglas more than I ever needed you in my whole entire life.' Magic said as she held her cat close to her heart while stroking its fur.

'How about I come over there and spend some time with you this morning when I shower and get dressed, around ten?' Douglas said wiping the sleep out of his eyes and slipping on a white tee keeping up with the latest fashion trend.

'Please be here, ten is fine. Wait until you hear what I want to talk to you about you gonna trip, this is some real shit Douglas, so please come and try to be on time.' Magic said this knowing how a thugs ten o'clock mean twelve or one o'clock in the afternoon if he made it at all.

"Ten it is baby, I won't let you down." Douglas said feeling the vibe once and for all.

'The trip will be well worth it. Have I ever led you wrong Magic said before hanging up the phone. She kissed her cat before setting it free. She knew in order for a dream to come true a person had to make the first step and the rest would fall into place. This was fact she had witnessed this so many times before, not to mention the old people always told her this all her life and she was ready to do what it would take to evolve.

'One down.' Magic said to herself feeling more confident and sexy but all was not well because in order to carry out a heist. Each and everybody involved had to have skills to carry it out like Band E skills like some of the greats who all went before her and the other who had not yet sealed their destinies confidence was something she wasn't lacking. Magic went to her bathroom to shower until Douglas came over the next morning to talk to her. A loud knock was at the door. She practically jumped out of bed to answer it with nothing on but a pair of sexy undies and a wife beater top. She hopped over the arm of the couch to get to the door because of the cluttered house.

'Hi baby.' Douglas said as he walked inside holding two coffees and a paper in his hands smelling like adidas urban spice cologne. The smell was so loud it lingered in the air and up Magic nostrils like a vapor.

'Glad you made it.' Magic said as she stepped to the side and let Douglas in.

'I couldn't stop thinking about you since you called me at five o'clock in the morning what is it that you want to ask me that's so urgent you couldn't wait until morning to call me?' Douglas asks as he propped his sexy brown ass on her brand new comforter.

'Douglas I'm tired of living like this look around you. I can't move around in my own apartment the place is so cluttered shit and the club is getting so outrageous our manager done went and started a touchy feely night where all these strange men get to touch our bodies. I left there last night and I'm not going to return. The dog thinks he fired me, but I quit.'

Douglas scratched his head hoping this was not the reason Magic broke his sleep in the wee hours of the morning.

And you want me too go down there and bust him up is that it, because if it is I'll do anything for you baby with your fine self, come here.' Douglas went to grab Magic and she pushed him back. He almost broke his neck flipping backward landing on Magic's pull out couch bed.

'Stop, Douglas I'm not playing this is serious.' Magic said grabbing a robe to throw over her bare brown skin feeling the feelings of coldness on her flesh. Her bright red hair and Japanese letters on her neck that spelled out her name was hypnotizing to Douglas. Every word that came out her mouth would be followed like a direct order.

'I don't want you to go to the club and do nothing to nobody, that club is history in my life. I have better plans and I need you to help me carry this plan out because it's a sure fire winner I haven't been tricking and dancing all my life for nothing. I learned a lot from the men I seduced.' Magic explained as a bolt of confidence rushed through her veins she was sure of herself at this moment and nothing would change her mind.

Douglas sat up at attention wondering what his friend was talking about he knew how scandalous dancers could be. But this particular one has something up her sleeve and he couldn't wait to hear what it was. Magic took a seat on the edge of the bed since it was in the living room blocking the entrance to the kitchen making life hard to get from one room to another.

'I just can't take any more bullshit man. You just don't know, this lifestyle is getting real tight. The money I make go straight from my garter belt to the rent man, and then after I pay the dog-he always ask me for some sex and the bills are so high I can't afford to stay here any longer. My Audi TT was a gift. That's the only thing I have to show what I'm worth and luckily one of my admirers gave it to me because it makes me look good when ever I'm seen in it." Magic expressed fear of asking Douglas the question that was burning a hole in her head.

'What do you want to ask me Magic? I can't sit here all day and listen to your problems because I have my own problems and if I start giving you a rundown you might think I'm less of a man. I can't do the things I want to do for the special people in my life, like my kids, what you think a woman is the only person allowed to live from hand to mouth men live that way too. I owe my son's mother around fifteen thousand dollars in back child support payments and I can't afford to pay her. When a thug looks for a job I can't find one. So I resorted to selling drugs and when that didn't work I do what I can to make ends meet, so what's up? I have a job to look for this morning" Douglas said knowing that the construction for a new jail was in the making. He knew if he didn't find a job soon, his next step would be right where the man wanted him. To see him keeping the correction officers employed.

'Douglas remember the last time we were together you told me you had a knack for taking electronics apart and putting them back together again. I actually saw you do this with my own eyes. Well I think I found the job that will make both our ends meet.' Magic said as she moved a little closer to Doug waiting for his response.

Douglas couldn't wait to hear what Magic was talking about. He knew she had an enterprising mind and a body to match. The deepest beauty of the white chocolate family this was Magic's appearance 38-24-38 if the commodores told it in one of there famous songs, a body like that would make the weakest brother beg for mercy this was Magic.

'What is it?' Douglas asks as he moved just as close with more than a job on his mind he was hoping for a little conciliation prize while acting enthused by this plan he was about to hear.

'Before I bust this bubble with you Douglas I need to know that this conversation will not leave this room because this shit could put us under the jail.' Magic said as she parted her legs waiting to hear if the thug who she wanted as a partner would break and do her will and bidding.

'You got my full trust and undivided attention.' Douglas said as his heart beat faster still waiting for the bubble to burst.

'Good, that is exactly what. I'll need is your undivided attention. After the plea for attention Magic finally broke the news, she whispered in Douglas ear knowing that in the ghetto the walls have ears; if she spoke too loud her plan would be street news in a matter of minutes and spread from one end of the ghetto to the next.

'I can't understand what you just said in my ear! You'll have to talk a little bit louder.' Douglas said as he took his hand and rubbed Magic thighs.

'I can show you better then I can tell you wait right here until I get dressed.' Magic said as she grabbed a pair of jeans off the top of a pile of clothes on the floor and squeezed her high maintenance body inside them, they fit like a glove just like she liked to show all her goodies in the imprints of her Rocawear Jeans.

'Don't ask me no question until I show you what I'm talking about, this is beyond your imagination.' Magic said knowing she was the bomb for coming up with a plan that would get them paid once and for all. Magic and Douglas took off in her Audi TT at high speed through the streets of ATL headed to the City on the interstate she had a "I'm on a mission" look in her eyes not caring what people thought of her at this point she just knew she wasn't willing to die a slave to the tight ass system of this world. She was a true gangsta in her eyes for going through life thus far in the conditions she lived under from the roach infested tenements and a life full of stone cold child abuse and foster homes was all she knew in the dark hidden ruins of her heart and at last she would finally be set free this was her secret thoughts. The car came to a sudden stop on the NE side of Atlanta, Georgia right in front one of the hottest jewelry stores in the mitts of Georgia's ATL." This is it." Magic said turning around looking in the window as the display was being took down and a new one set up with all kinds of diamond studded jewelry this was a special showing of some expensive diamonds in their region and she wanted them all. Greed was the name of this game. If she was ever going to get out of the hood this would be the only way and going out in style was her plan. She knew at this point that the job would go down, there was no doubt in her mind, and things were looking up.

'A jewelry store, what is it about this store? Do you want me to marry you or something? Is that why you brought me here to buy the ring is that it? Well I got news for you I can't afford it right now.' Douglas said with a less than a man look in his face.

'First of all what I'm about to say is serious this is not a joke so I want you to take me very serious. Douglas and no I don't want to marry you I'm about to put you down with some raw shit and I need you to use all the special skills you have in your body to do this for me; I want you to help me rip this bitch off.' Magic said looking devious and dead serious without a smile on her face. She knew what it felt like to be cold and hungry and without a job in one of ATL most prestigious go-go joints and she had no skills for a suitable future.

'You can't be serious.' Douglas said as he laughed gazing over his shoulder at the store window as the workers looked on.

'I couldn't be more serious then I am right now. Doug, I need your electronic expertise to help me trip the alarms long enough to grab some of those diamonds in the showcases, If you ever wanted to do anything in your life worth something this should be it.'

'Shit if your going to do this do it right why go for the little stuff like you said this is it, if this is to be done it will have to be done right with detail and expertise.' Douglas said as he turned around in his seat casing the joint out looking for the easiest way in. He never imagined this lurking in the mind of a delicate sexy flower like Magic he seen her as a dancer with a fabulous body that ever man desired not the gangsta she projected her self to be. He knew that desperate times was upon both of them and she couldn't be more right he needed money there was no in, and or but about it.

'Look there is no way your getting in that store through the front door they have gates and a serious alarm system, its going to be impossible. The alarm system probably looks like the matrix in there after dark. Look at the workers, don't those bitches look happy. They feel secure knowing what I say is true." Douglas said as his partner in crime turned her head looking in the window seeing the point Douglas had just made.

'Are you saying it can't be done, Douglas?' Magic asks with a look of concern on her face, she didn't want to believe this not by a long shot.

"Oh Yeah, it can be done but in a better way". Douglas expressed putting his silly side away. He knew if he was going to be involved this would be an opportunity to show a woman he really liked that he was all man and a real thug at heart and there was no other women he wanted to show this to but Magic, but she just didn't know it yet. He planned on unleashing his feeling before the job was done.

"Your brilliant, look at you, I'm glad I called you", Magic said parting her legs looking sexier than ever in her jeans and sexy top. Douglas had to let her know how he felt if it was the last thing he did, his confidence was shot at this moment.

'I can get you in and out of there in a matter of seconds with the right tools and people backing me. There is no way we can do this alone are you feeling me, first of all the alarm system is state of the art and second of all your not bonafied or qualified to carry out a plan like this on your own.' Douglas said as he looked up to the roof of the store calculating in his mind the ends and out of things.

'That's impossible, how can you do this, Douglas?' Magic asks knowing all she knew about robbery was the shit she seen on television. Douglas could not be more right about this point he had just made. She just wanted it all that was the motivation that moved her to commit a state of suicide, which was to come. Greed, lust, desire, want, this was the feeling that ran through her veins.

13

Douglas pointed to the roof and the store next door which was a famous soul food restaurant that didn't close until two o'clock in the morning. He knew if they were to do this it would have to be in the wee hours of the morning.

'Let's get our black asses from in front of the store before a cop come along and that's the last thing I need right now. There is no telling what I would do to save myself and you. Last night I couldn't help but stop here on the way home from work and I was ask by a cop what I was doing just because he seen I'm an African American women hanging around a jewelry store after hours.' Magic said.

Douglas just listened and continued to calculate the new plans in his mind not to mention the fact that Magic had just expressed her feelings to him. She told him she didn't know what she would do if the police would come after them if they were to get caught she'd become a true gangsta like the peoples she lived around all her life. This was an epidemic that seems to hit the ghetto. Everyday money was needed to survive there was no way around this fact, if you wanted to eat you needed money, if you wanted sex you needed money, to lay down in a warm house or apartment at night you needed money. This is what ran through Douglas mind and it was the truth, he was tired of not being able to send his children a child support check every month on time like he wished he could. Shit was hard but he bared a smile on his face everyday anyway and gamed and played his way through life. It was hard not bursting out in tear being a full grown man and all. When you choose to be a thug society viewed him in a negative light anyway so he decided to be down with the heist hoping everything went as planned because money wouldn't be handed to him on a silver platter or jobs in that matter especially the jobs that would bring in real money without becoming a slave to society.

'Damn, Douglas we'll need some back up we can't do this shit by ourselves, like a look out man you know, somebody to help us grab the shit all those diamond especially the pink ones, because their worth a pretty penny, what do you think?' Magic asks cruising down the interstate driving anywhere just as long as the plan was in the making a talk was necessary in order for the plan to come to the light.

'Damn right I have just the two people that can help us I have a cousin that's here from New York City where all the real gangsta dwell. He's exactly what we need right now he would love this shit.'

'I don't just want anybody; I need nigga's with skills who know what the fuck their doing. Can you find me a couple of skillful men to be down with this? The payoff will be all the diamonds your ass can carry and once we get them we have to find a way to liquidate them can you dig it.' Magic said feeling like the queen she wanted to become.

'I can't wait I need money now! My damn bills are taking over my life not to mention money I owe out from past credit cards debt. My world is just about to explode. If we don't do this I might as well commit suicide' Magic said with a tear sparkling in the corner of her eye. Looking down at her privates she was tired of stripping and living life like a ho. This was not the way she was raised. Why should her life end up like this, all the parties was just about played out in her mind. The next party she wanted to attend she wanted to take place in one of those fly mansion in Hampton Georgia like some of those fly ass girls that danced at the club with the business men licking them from head to toe every night it seemed like all the fly one's were taken when she stepped foot in town. From Compton California to Miami Florida she flocked to Georgia because she had heard so much about the strip clubs there. She was told money was running in the streets, this is what attracted her to this town and her friend Gee-Gee; she was Magic's

15

world and best friend in life. They had been through all the same styles of child of abuse and could share stories with one another to cleanse themselves of some of the junk they stored in their truck of the memories who made them who they are today strippers.

Take me back to the hood and I'll be in touch tonight with information of who will be down with us and who won't. Douglas said feeling a sense of control running through his veins he would be set on high if all was to go as planned. Child support would be taken care of no doubt, not to mention the things he felt cheated out of all of his life. This would restore what he felt was stolen.

'What happened to my 6 acres and a mule?' Douglas said looking desperate in the face, while Magic continued talking laying out all the ground rules.

'Don't have me sitting by the phone and your black behind don't call. I'm trusting you with this. You can't be telling a whole lot of people what we're about to do, Douglas don't let me down.' Magic said as she worried he would tell some of the wrong people in the hood and they'd end up getting popped and that person would just so happen end up getting paid but not from the heist but by the police for turning them in this seemed to be the down fall of all the people Magic knew who are doing time in prison. Somebody always turn a brother or a sista in for their own selfish gains.

'Have I ever let you down, Magic?' Douglas asks as he looked her deep in the eyes before leaning over and kissing her on the cheek and thanking her for saving his life.

'You never cease to amaze me with your slick ass Magic; you came to me with this heist plan at a time in life when I would do just about anything to survive some of the shit that falls in my lap.' Douglas said as Magic cruised through the streets about to drop him off in the hood so he could find the perfect people that fit the criteria for the plan to take place.

Night quickly came as Magic sat by the phone stoking her cat Blossom waiting for the call that would change her life forever. This made her nervous she had a nervous stomach just thinking about it. The phone begins to ring she stared at it afraid to pick it up knowing this phone call would turn her destiny in a whole nother direction. Knowing what was about to be said would change her life for ever either for the better or for the worst destiny was so full of surprises and she hoped everything she wanted to do would come to a desired end and everyone would live happy ever after and rich as Jay-Z with the fringe benefits that were to come.

'Hello.' Magic said in a soft mellow voice into the receiver of her cell phone.

'Magic it's on I got two good guys to back us up tonight you best be believing that, hunger run rapid in these streets as if you didn't know.' Douglas said.

"Get over here Douglas. I don't want to talk about this over the phone it's dangerous' Magic yelled before slamming the receiver down as her heart jumped because shit was falling into place. The only uneasy feeling she felt was the one that led Douglas out into the streets to find the ones who was their so called back.

Magic pulled out a bottle of cheap champagne; and popped two valiums in her mouth there was a knock on the door. By this time the bottle of champagne was halfway empty.

"Who is it?" She yelled feeling light headed from drinking and the over dose of valium. She had just played Russian roulette with her life, hoping deep inside this would end it for real for real deep in her subconscious mind she was ready to cross over death or wealth one would out rule the other in the end of things she prayed for the riches she wasn't quit ready for death to come along and claim her sexy youthful body but the finances just was not there.

'It's me partner.' Douglas yelled through the door in a happy voice

Magic opened the door and stepped to the side to let a bunch of stranger who was to bring the plan that lurk in her mind to the source of light but trust had to be established in order to feel secure.

"Who is this? Douglas." Magic asks with concern in her voice and on her face the look was obvious.

She checked out the clothing and shoes of the unknown stranger Douglas had just brought into her life. They looked authentic they didn't wear cop shoes and they looked like stone cold gangster from the hood. The feeling of hate crossed her mind but in order to get what she wanted trust was an issue.

'Who are they?' Magic asks hoping they would be able to help her penetrate the walls of the jewelry store in order to get the spoils.

"This here is the man, not just any man he's the one who's going to get us in and out in a matter of seconds and this guy here he's the one who's going to watch our backs while we grab all the diamonds." Douglas said as he picked up the bottle of cheap champagne and turned the bottle up to his mouth wiping off any excess that dripped down his chin with his hand.

"And how is this, they don't look as if they could penetrate me, so how are they going to penetrate some walls. Magic ask seated on the arm of her chair.

"I'm Kevin and he's my cousin James can we sit down?" Kevin asks as he sat on the arm of the couch smiling at Magic.

"Douglas what's going on here and why did you bring them here tonight I thought we had an understanding." Magic said mad as hell but not showing it.

18

"Kevin has all the right tools needed for this job Magic, that's why I brought him here."

"I don't know why you would bring them here!" Magic ask as she looked Douglas friend over from head to toe knowing deep in her heart that he would be trouble.

"Listen if you really want to do this you're going to have to trust me that is very necessary. We also have the right tools to get the job done, show her the tools, man." Douglas said at this point Kevin pulled out his workman's pouch he pulled out a chisel and a variety of other gadgets.

"First of all Miss I don't want to go through the motions either you want to hit this jewelry store or what if so I'm here to help I have all the necessary gadget it will take, the only question is when do you want to carry this plan out, tonight? Kevin asks.

"How in the hell are we going to carry this out in one night especially when we haven't even been over the plans yet!" Magic said.

"Listen I been doing smash and grabs seems like forever I don't need no women telling me how I need to do my job. I'm telling you what needs to be done, Douglas explained the store front to me and if you want to go and stake the joint out we can do that too it doesn't matter to me I'll still be down." Kevin expressed sitting there in his tugged out Gucci wear.

"I was thinking I could go in and see how the security system is set up and from there we'll know how to move." Magic said feeling a bolt of power rush through her veins.

"That sounds logical." Kevin said.

"So what is his job function?" Magic asks as she pointed to the big black thug with the dew rag on his head that looked as if he came straight from the corner.

"He's one of the look out men, him and Douglas will take turns looking out."

"Answer me this question why do they need to take turns looking out especially since you claim you can get us in and out in a matter of seconds." Magic asks as she searched Kevin's face for the answer as she looked around at each one of the men who were about to carryout her dream plan.

"Damn, I must be freaking loosing my mind. Look at them! "Magic said to herself as she reached for the bottle of champagne to wash down another valium pill.

"Let the games begin, get yourself together we're going down there and case the joint out." Kevin announced.

"Why?" Magic ask not feeling it but feeling a pharmaceutical high instead.

"I want to know what I'm getting my self into Miss Lady, and doesn't anybody in this group have my back like I have my own back so get up and get a move on." Kevin announced showing Magic his true thuggish side and she liked it.

"So you claim you know exactly what to do and that right there makes me feel more confident. That's just what I've been waiting for." Magic said as she moved closer to him while he gazed her down from head to toe, Douglas acts like he owned the rights to Magic he became quit jealous.

"Let's start planning isn't that what we are here for?" Douglas asks.

"Have you guys been down there yet?" Magic ask seeing if Douglas defied her trust. She didn't want the plan spread from NE to SW Georgia. She knew how some men could be from catering to them for so long. Networking was something Georgian's were famous for.

"No, we haven't been nowhere near the crime scene just yet." Kevin said while smiling at Magic.

"Crime scene, that place aint no crime scene yet. Once we're finished, it will be a total land mark."

Magic said naïve to the crime and charges B and E could bring with them.

"I have your back." James said knowing the ends and the out's of robbery of a jewelry store. He knew they could have been shot and killed during the whole operation. He knew when one person fell the others weren't far behind.

"And what is your expertise?" Magic ask James with suspicion in her voice.

"I'm good at watching a nigga's back. That all I have to know because where we are about to go there is no turning back, this is some real mafia shit getting ready to take place. The only thing that we have to do now is find out where we are going to turn our treasures to cash, because that's what we are going to need in order for shit to go right, cash." All the gangsta's in the room gave each other high five.

"While you're asking us what our experience is how about you what do you know how to do? Kevin asked looking like curious George waiting for an answer to his question.

"I'm the one who found the store; I'm the one who let Douglas in on it." All eyes turned in Douglas direction thinking he was the master mind behind the plan.

"No, Douglas is not the master mind I am and if you want to be down with my plan, you will have to follow my orders. The heist will take place tomorrow night in the wee hours of the morning when the streets are clear and all club are closed." Magic expressed.

"Why do all the clubs have to be closed?" Douglas asks.

"Because all the clubs are on that side of town and they all close at two or three o'clock in the morning, mastermind." Magic said looking the man she trusted with her dream in the eyes he led the two guys who was to bring everything to the light to believe he was the one who came up with the master plan.

"So when will we be going down to stake the joint out?" James asks holding the chisel in his hand ready to break into something.

"Do y'all think tonight would be better." Douglas asks.

"Tonight it is then, but before we go I just want to say this is a life or death situation about to go down here and I need to know I can trust all of you and I also need to know when the job is done you will not run and tell your momma's, sisters, girlfriends, I also need to know where you guy's live." Magic said as if she was the leader of a club and these gangsta's were her member's.

"Fuck all that Mickey Mouse club bullshit put your clothes on and let's go." Kevin said.

"Why are you in such a rush to do the job?" Magic asks.

"Money baby money now you do the math." Kevin said looking dead serious before opening the front door to Magic house walking out to his Mercedes SL 550

Magic was surprised he drove such an expensive car.

"I have to talk to Douglas in private before we go." Magic explained to her new found crew.

"No problem, but you two let get going afterward time is a very important matter in robbery." Kevin exclaimed.

Magic liked Kevin he reminded her of a fifty cent, smart, slick, quite, but knew how to get what he wanted; the only noise he made while in her present was the noise of a cash register coughing up the cash.

Kevin and James got in the car waiting for the one who brought this necessary mess into their lives.

"I like that Kevin, but who is that other nigga?" Magic ask looking at Doug like he was crazy.

"You told me to trust you which I did; I did what you ask me too when you called me at five o'clock in the morning or do you have amnesia now?" Douglas asks.

"I just want to make sure we don't get popped that's all I don't want to go to jail." Magic explained.

"I don't want to go to jail either but if shit seem like it might back fire run for your black ass life because no matter who we trust with this the police is the only one who I know who can change lives." Douglas said

"I love money and I want those diamond and what ever other jewelry we might so happen to pick up but hell if I would sacrifice my freedom for them, if the police do come you be sure to tell your little tugged out friend not to snitch on who ever might get caught."

"No doubt Magic this is a done deal." As the two were talking Kevin blew the horn knowing how precious time could be, doing time in the prison system this is what he learned doing twelve years from age sixteen to being twenty six when those door of the state prison opened up and spewed him out. He made a vow with himself to take the streets by storm to boost his ego and prove he still had what it take to make it even if it took robbing, stealing, and killing to do it. Robbery was nothing to men like Douglas, James, and Kevin they spent their whole live trying to be the men they thought their mother would love, a man to take charge even if the streets was the only place the white man would let a brother do, the schools, and the jails this was all they knew, the streets was for the taking no matter how many niggas claimed this or that turf was theirs, if it took killing to get what they wanted they were willing to do it. James and his brother Sammy been doing jobs for ever or so it seemed. he never been caught and he planned on not getting caught this night, that was the last thing on his mind this plan would help him take ATL by storm and get the car of his dreams, diamonds where worth a lot in his mind and if he could confiscate enough to make something of himself and look big to the ladies so be it even if it meant killing people who stepped in his way whether wearing a uniform or not.

As the Mercedes SL 550 cruised the interstate to the spot in time where destiny was to be made and history all in the same breath. The car exited the streets down a dark spiral road and came to a complete stOp.

"What's going on Kevin, why did you stop?" Magic and the others ask.

"I just thought I should let each one of y'all know if we just so happen to get popped and one of y'all snitch my name out your mouth I will find you." Kevin made the sign of an invisible gun and blew the tip of the smoking make believe gun hoping his point was being made.

"I feel the same way." James blurted out.

"Me too." Said Magic

"Just because I'm a girl don't mean I can't roll with the best of them and if my name or location just so happen to roll off one of y'all lips I'll have you killed." Magic explained.

"Douglas sat there in silence then he started talking." I feel y'all." Douglas said.

"I just want to get this shit over with that all so let get moving, start the car."

Kevin did as ordered as the car continued down the dark highway headed to the jewelry store that would make or break Magic and her crew.

"Pull around that corner over there, that's where the store is." Magic yelled.

As the Mercedes turned the corner James pulled out his black bandanna and tied it around his mouth trying to conceal his identity. The only way he knew how and that was to look gangsta this was the only thing he knew that would strike fear in the hearts of men and he would-be the one to represent the call to gangsterism.

The doors to the car swung open as the car came to a complete stop in front of the most beautiful window display of diamond that Magic had ever seen.

"This shit is better than the other diamonds I wanted. Grab all these bitches." Magic express as she ran her bow-legs around the corner in the alley way near the back entrance to the jewelry store.

Magic was just about to push the door trying to see if the alarm would go off if she just touches it.

"This is no time for games if you touch that door we might as well pack it up and return home because that will trigger all the alarms, I can see now I'm going to have to keep my eyes on you." Kevin explained stepping into a black overall outfit while tying a bandana around his mouth to conceal his identity just as his partner James had done.

"Just get me inside so we can get the hell out of here!" Magic said scared deep down in her heart, really not knowing what she was doing or what to expect.

"I have to climb up to the roof and me and James will have the door open in a matter of minute." Kevin explained as he climbed up the side of the building like spider man.

"I sure want to know how in the hell are you two going to do that considering the roof is so thick how can you blow a hole in there so fast." Magic asks shocked at the claim Kevin made about having a spot open wide enough for them to climb in.

"I told you I knew what I was doing Magic, these niggas are real gangsta's." Douglas expressed as he stood there trying his hardest to appear gangster but all the while being an imitation by rights.

"Yeah...yeah...yeah...Magic said as her and Douglas stood there waiting for their cue to enter the store.

"This heist is going to put us on the map, Douglas thank you for finding us a couple of geniuses to get us in." Magic gave Douglas a hug as they stood on the side of the building in an alleyway patiently waiting...

"I see Kevin seems to like you." Douglas expressed.

"Oh, hells no don't stand out here and ruin my dream with this bull shit, who cares if Kevin like me what man don't like me. Kevin is going to get me in here where all the jewels are so back off and let's get to work." Magic said.

Kevin gave his cue and Magic and Douglas climbed up a stringed latter to get to the top of the roof where the two ex-cons with heist experience sat waiting for their partners one by one.

The store was dark they all lowered themselves down to enter, Douglas was the last one down, Kevin pulled out three black plastic bags handing his protégés one.

"Grab all the shit you can like there's no tomorrow because for real if we get caught there won't be." Kevin explained.

"There is no tomorrow as far as I'm concerned, if this doesn't work I might as well be dead." Douglas said.

"It's working fool be quite and grab." Magic whispered with fear running through her heart and bells ringing in her ears.

"Hurry up because the alarm will come back on in a couple of minutes and if we're not out of here we will get caught, I'm going to share this with you grab all the gold you can because that can be smelted down and sold by the bars." Kevin said.

"Yeah that's a smart idea." Magic said with all the diamonds she seen in the pink ice window display in her bag. Just as the two were talking Douglas took a hammer and smashed the window display into pieces and glass flew everywhere including Magic's eyes, she dropped her bag and started to rub them as blood seeped down the front of her face to her clothes. Drops of blood landed on the floor creating another problem.

"Are you crazy fool you going to get us popped?" Kevin yelled in a loud whisper.

The pain got so intense Magic begun to cry and the blood flowed worst she hoped she would be able to see again because it was quit impossible with glass in her eyes.

"Let's get the hell out of here I hear the police sirens coming grab the bags Magic are you alright baby?" Kevin asks

"I don't know I can't see." Magic became hysterical she didn't care about money or diamonds at this point. She just knew she couldn't see and wanted to get out of the store in one piece without getting shot by the police.

"James helps Magic to the roof so we can get out of here and you Douglas I have a bone to pick with you when we get back around the way." Kevin said with a strike of hate in his heart for bringing this inexperience nigga with him on a heist in the first place.

James grabbed Magic around the shoulders and guided her up the shaky rope to climb to the top without falling the sirens were getting closer and closer as they made way to the Mercedes and they spun off in to the night.

Kevin pulled his bandana off and James did the same, they wanted to shoot Douglas for fucking up.

"I knew I shouldn't have brought you in the store with us, look at the mess you made. If you would have stuck to the plan the heist wouldn't have got messy, now look we got
Half the shit we could have gotten." Kevin pulled his gun out of his pants holding it to Douglas temple.

"I know the cops are coming looking for us now, all because of you there's no telling if Magic left some blood behind there was no time to check." Kevin explained to Americas dumbest criminal Douglas.

"I need to go to the hospital, I can't see!" Magic said scared of the outcome of her plans to grab the loot and get the spoils.

"You ruined everything Douglas are you stupid or what look at me now; I can't even see what's in front of me!"

"We got a lot of shit here y'all." James said looking in each bag as they drove down the interstate doing a hundred miles per hour.

"I think you need to slow down or you're going to attract the police." Douglas said feeling dumb inside for ruining everything. He knew he had lost his friend Magic at this moment and didn't think she would be coming back.

"Just let me out right here!" Douglas said as his demons rose up inside of him.

"What are you talking about man, what you mean let you out right here?" Kevin asks slowing down.

Douglas pushed the door open with his shoulder as he grabbed hold of his bag and walked away from the Mercedes. Kevin started to cruise beside him to give him a little speech before he walked into the night.

"Let me hear something in the street with my name attached to it, I will be coming for you man and I guaranteed you this." Kevin looked at him with a hard core look on his face before driving off. Magic laid on the back seat with her eyes burning.

"I'm taking you home with me tonight. I will help you with getting the glass out your eyes." Kevin said.

Magic held her bag of diamond so tight not trusting any body near them.

"At least you got what you wanted out the deal before you got hurt, where exactly did you meet that clown shorty?" Kevin asks concerning Douglas.

"I met him at the club years ago. What Club? A club I worked at stripping. He came in and we hit it off almost immediately I never known he was this way. He acted as if he knew how to hit the joint up when I told him my plan."

"That nigga don't know nothing he never even paid a bill in his life." Kevin said.

"Don't you know a gangsta when you see one shorty?" James asks.

"I wasn't thinking like that when I ask for his help I was just thinking about getting the jewels that's all." Magic said.

The Mercedes pulled up to James residence he jumped out the car vowing to meet up with his partners in crime for a break down of the merchandise in the morning.

"No matter what y'all say about Douglas even though he almost put my eyes out he did try to help me with this, I would have never met you if he hadn't introduce me to you." Magic said.

"True." Kevin said as he pulled Magic closer to him and took a napkin to pat her eyes hoping to ease the pain.

""Did you think any of the blood got on the floor when I started bleeding? Magic asks.

CHAPTER 2

The Heist, Part II

"At least you got what you wanted out of the deal before you got hurt, I just want to know where exactly did you meet that clown, shorty?" Kevin asks as he cruised down the interstate headed to his place.

"I met him at the club." Magic said.

"What club if you don't mind me asking?" Kevin asks.

"I met him at Stroker's along time ago. I didn't know he was this way because when I gave him a run down of the floor plans he acts as if he was an expert with skills to hit up the joint." Magic explained.

"That nigga don't know nothing he never even paid a bill in his life, don't you know a true gangsta when you see one." Kevin asks.

"I wasn't thinking like that when I ask him to help me pull this shit off I just wanted to get the jewels that's all.' Magic explained.

The Mercedes pulled up to the front door of James residence. He lived in a flat near the scene he jumped out of the car holding his spoils tight looking over his shoulder making sure no body was clocking his moves. As he moved real smooth away from the car he turned around and assured his friends he would get up with them the following day to find a liquidator.

"No matter what y'all say about Douglas even though he almost put my eye out, he tried to help me with this, there's no doubt about that and I hope he's not mad at me, the only good thing besides these jewel is I'm glad he introduced me to you." Magic said.

"True." Kevin whispered.

"Do you think any blood got on the floor at the scene, Kevin?" Magic asks.

"Hell, no and even if it did, how would you feel if I ask you to bring your fine ass with me to New York?" Kevin asked

"I hardly even know you." Magic said trying to feel where Kevin was coming from since her eyes was unable to gaze upon his fine dark frame.

"I like you and I don't unusually go around asking females to go nowhere with me but you baby and me together could hurt something.' Kevin explained.

"I like you too." Magic said not quit sure of herself.

"I don't know about that Douglas character he remind me of one of those dukie nigga's. A nigga like that would turn you and his diamonds over to the police to look like a hero." Kevin explained.

"He told me you were his cousin." Magic said trying to find out the truth from Kevin.

"Do we look like cousins?" Kevin asked.

"Now that you brought it up no he doesn't look nothing like you."

The Mercedes pulled up to a slick house sitting on what looked like a mountain top. The house was so well put together it looked as if an architect took special pride and interest in building it.

"Come on in here and let me help you feel better." Kevin said as he helped Magic in the front door, her diamonds were clutched under her arms as she entered the house.

"I appreciate this for real." Magic said not knowing what the house looked like because her eyes were locked shut.

"Come in the bathroom and let's wash this shit out your eyes with some eye wash." Kevin took Magic into the bathroom she laid the bag of diamonds on the toilet top and took hold of the bottle and begun to wash her eyes out, as she patted her face dry afterward she opened her eyes and Kevin stood behind her ready to assist in anyway he could.

"Wow that feels a hundred times better." Magic said with a sigh of relief.

"I figured it would." Kevin replied as he guides Magic into the living room holding her hand.

She followed his lead plotting in her mind all the while she hadn't a clue as to where to take the jewels and liquidate them so she could be swimming in doe, which is where this plan was suppose to take her.

"Hey, Kevin I have a question?" Magic said.

"Shoot." Kevin said.

"Do you think we will be able to get money quick for these?" Magic ask as she took her big black plastic bag and dumped the content onto the rug as she did a stooped dip down over them.

"Absolutely." Kevin said calculating in his mind the future outcome of his unparticular plot.

"Where?" Magic asked.

"That's why it necessary we take a little trip."

"A trip to New York?" Magic asked.

"You know it. I have connections in that direction, and I just bounced down here as a retreat just waiting for some of the noise I left up top to calm down, as if you didn't notice I have all I need this is just a sport to me baby."

Magic looked around her to see what lied beyond this fly structured world she was lured into by this fly by night thug. He had her weak in the knees his ways was smooth to her she loved it. He couldn't deny his feeling in front of her either her persona made him melt the jewels laid there in the middle of the floor as Magic picked up a big pink diamond ring and slid it on her finger it fit perfectly, she felt like the princess she always dreamt of being, then Kevin pulled out two champagne glasses to celebrate their getting out of the jewelry store in one piece.

"This is worth celebrating baby; you're a genius I would have never known a go-go dancer could come up with this one here. I just thought y'all girl were into just making a nigga feel good you know, why else would a women want to bounce around in her g-strings twenty four seven."

"Is this supposed to be a compliment or a disc?" Magic asked as she sat on Kevin's pit styled couch looking out the back double door across the beautiful beach while holding a fist full of diamonds, this is exactly what she wanted and this nigga here had it all the lifestyle she craved.

"And look at you; you must have been doing this for years living like a king on top of a hill. I would have never known looking at you when Douglas brought you to my spot." Magic said as she smiled.

"That where a whole lot of female mess up, that's just why I don't have one by my side like I should. All y'all basically want to know is what a nigga is driving, where a nigga work, how much money a nigga is making, you see I'm full of surprises I live my life strictly on the edge and I love the fact that you remind me of myself that count for something." Kevin said.

"Come here Kevin I owe you this." Magic wet her lips and gave Kevin a wet long kiss; he made her dream come true. If she hadn't meet him who knows where she would have ended up and considering Douglas turned out to be total disappointment.

"Damn, girl." Kevin said as he backed up knowing he was in love at this point there was doubt about this. He wanted Magic to be his girl and he wouldn't stop until he had her just where he wanted her in his life.

"Can we calculate exactly what we have here, Kevin." Magic asks

Kevin walked in the kitchen and came out with a bottle expensive champagne, he poured Magic a glass as she laid all the jewelry out on the table

33

counting her pieces, she wasn't satisfied until she knew exactly how many pieces she had in her plastic bag.

"Forget that shorty, this is only the beginning you're rolling with me now." Kevin said as he tilted his glass up to his mouth, he looked sexy standing there as the light gazed across his ebony face. He was fine in Magic's eyes she liked the way he looked his goatee made him look wiser than any nigga she had seen lately. she had her share of men but this one there was something special about him she couldn't put her finger on it, he seemed to be knowledgeable she felt a sense of trust and you could move around in his living room with no problem. Why not give him a chance.

"I'm gonna tell you this, shorty if you stick with me your gonna be the riches female in ATL." Kevin said in a relax manner turning his glass up one more time sucking up the remainder of his champagne.

"How come you haven't dumped your bag yet?' Magic ask looking concerned at this moment.

"I already know what I picked up there's no need to keep looking at it again, I already know what I'm gonna get for them too." Kevin said sure of himself.

"How is this, I can't understand you, I been dreaming of living like this all my life and here you come wanting to be down with us so called dukie ass niggas. Are you the police?" Magic asks as she shoved all her fines in the bag and clutched it even harder.

Kevin laughed.

"It's alright you wouldn't be the first desperate female I ran across, I know times are tight and it's obvious you want more." Kevin said feeling Magic out looking at the expressions on her face as he talked.

"I'm not desperate. What are you talking about I just have some over due bills and the walls feel like they are about to close up on me that all." Magic said as she smirked still clutching the bag trying to sound sarcastic.

"You don't have to lie to me, baby, I will put you down with this if you want a piece there's enough money out here for all of us.

"What are you talking about Kevin?" Magic asked naive to game of B and E; she just went with what was in her heart.

"I have been doing smash and grab all my life. First I lived in Compton doing smash and grabs and a variety of other Cities.

"Excuse me for interrupting you, but you said you lived in Compton, I lived in Compton." Magic said feeling extra excited still paying close attention to what Kevin was about to saying.

"I want you to join me and traveling from state to state hitting up stores. What do you have to say about that?" Kevin asks knowing he just laid a whammy on Magic.

"You can't be serious!" Magic said.

"I been planning this for a long time now and it's time. I just feel it in my bones. This is the right season first of all, and I've been down too long for me not to know how the police roll. I was paying close attention to you tonight you move pretty swift and I like your style, I'm still shocked a female was bold enough to sit down and plot out a heist this is pretty impressive shit in my eyes (Kevin said laughing), I lived all over the place from Boston, to Compton, New York, Chicago, Miami, I laid in my cell one night and vowed to take back the shit that been robbed from me for years and now I want to bring this shit to the for front and to an conclusion." Kevin explained as he took the floor and made all kind of hand gestures trying to explain his plans to Magic to see if she was down by law or what.

"Sounds good to me, but who's gonna back us up. It seem like I always hit that note." Magic said.

"I got back and they got back bone believe me these are some hard core nigga's I'm talking about

New York made us that way, this shit we did tonight was like a Scooby snack to me." Kevin explained.

Kevin sat down besides Magic trying to get her to see the exact same picture he did. She finally did after hours of talking she was brain washed by the time Kevin finished with her.

The diamond drop was set up money would finally exchange hands and all was well as far as Magic was concerned. she would get to do some of the things she always wanted to do, after drinking for the remainder of the wee hours of the morning she finally gave in to a feeling she was having Kevin hadn't made no move except the kiss he complied with hours earlier.

"What you doing shorty?" Kevin ask as he sat there watching Magic de-stress she took off her outfit and stood there in the mist of his living room butter ball naked and tipsy from all the champagne.

"Can I trust you, Kevin?" Magic asked.

"Of course you can, shorty." Kevin said.

"Can I really?" Magic asks again as she slowly walked across the floor in his direction.

"Let me tell you something, shorty there is nothing you can tell me that I haven't all ready been through." Kevin explained.

"I use to be real poor and I hated it. I always hated the fact that my mother couldn't afford some of the things everybody else mother's could but it's not all about that I found out it all about being able to see straight through all the bull shit and I can." Kevin said.

"You can what?" Magic asked.

"I can see straight through bullshit. I can tell you this I'm willing to take all of the shit they cheated me out of all my life and if you want to be down then let me know right now. I'm sick of seeing my sista's struggling to survive and all the information they been cheated out of all their life why should you have to struggle." Kevin said

"I'm feeling you there. I was just talking about this same thing with Douglas before we plotted the hit tonight. I was telling him everybody think because I'm a dancer at a strip joint I'm rolling in the dough but my shit ain't nothing like they imagine, I owe my life out at least it feels that way. I feel like if I die and owe these paper chasers those bitches will come to the grave yard to collect so what ever the plan is you can put me down with it. Magic said before walking over to Kevin sitting down on his lap in the nude.

"First of all I want you to know something I like you but I don't want to do you. I want our relationship to be strictly business no sex." Kevin said busting Magic's bubble

She couldn't believe a thug passing up some pussy, how odd.

"In two days we will be headed to the East Coast, so pack your shit." Kevin explained.

"The East Coast, huh." Magic followed orders she wasn't going to argue with the nigga that got her in and out of the Jewelry store. She pasted by ever night for weeks plotting the hit. He was a knight in shining armor in her eyes. She still was in shock from everything moving so fast but in the back of her mind she wondered what Douglas was doing, she could tell he was pissed when he walked away into the night. She hoped when he cashed his spoils in he would get enough money to pay his over due child support he complained about so much. She felt him she felt that was the reason they clicked so well. She hoped he didn't think she was mad at him for breaking the showcase and glass getting it in her eyes making them sprinkle a little blood. She figured the proposal Kevin made was right up her alley after all it was summer time and this was the time to get the winter harvest and lay back living while the snow and cold winds blew.

"Tomorrow we are going to fly into the City. I want you to meet my boy's we cleared lots of heist together."

"Damn this is a little bit deeper then what I was looking for, all I wanted was to get the diamonds cash them in and live large you know blend in." Magic explained.

"Blend in and how are you planning on doing that?" Kevin said giggling.

"It can be done I'm the queen of blending in ask any of those female down at the club they'll tell you Magic can blend in very well, I was planning on liquidating the diamonds and getting me a much bigger place so me and my cat could have some room to move around once and for all, my apartment is so small I can't get to one room with out having to climb over something I'm sure you noticed that when you were there." Magic said looking Kevin deep in the eyes.

"Yeah that's cute." Kevin said.

This dude was a whole lot different from all the other guys she had ever met he wanted her to be one of his down by law heist partners, damn this was big. She couldn't count the dollar bills floating around in her head fast enough, she wanted to be down but what was her job function going to be she wondered.

The night quickly passed time was not like the norm each and ever minute of the day mattered in Kevin's mind. He made the most of each minute before she could get up he had took all the diamonds and had them liquidated. When Magic woke up out of her drunken sleep she awoke to five stacks of hundred dollar bills.

They were stack up nicely on the table waiting for her to open her eyes. She did and jumped up and grabbed them with a big wide smile on her face.

"That what you wanted isn't it?" Kevin asks as he opened a bag unleashing it content on the table.

"Damn, right this is what I wanted, I love you." Magic screamed as she danced around the room like a teenaged school girl. She couldn't believe he found the connection he claimed he didn't have.

She stopped dancing after she thought about it Kevin stood there with his hand on his goatee pulling on the hair watching his newfound friend reaction to the skits of what was to come. He liked to see a hungry chick gloat over money. he knew he could make her into what ever it was he wanted anything and take her anywhere he wanted too this is where control came in.

"You act as if you never seen that much money before. I can't believe that with you being so beautiful and all. I know those guys down at Stroker's have to gloat over you like your gloating over all that money." Kevin replied as he stood there still stroking his goatee as he watched Magic she was Magic to his eyes laying there amazed by each and everything he did for her and to her she loved it. He could tell all this in twenty four hours he didn't know how to act.

His cell phone started to ring.

"Who's this?" He asks when he answered it.

"Starky, what's up man, we'll be in town tomorrow and I'm bringing my girl with me." Kevin said in the receiver of his phone like a stone cold New Yorker.

Magic listened in.

"Make sure everybody's there man." Kevin said before hanging up.

"Who was that? That there was the rest of my crew tomorrow when we hit town we have a job to do we move fast when it's this time of the season. shits wide open for us and if we take it all is well do you understand where I'm coming from Magic?" Magic looked dumbfounded she didn't understand a word coming out of Kevin's mouth, he was sure not talking B and E and this was not her world she just wanted a taste of it not the whole thing. Kevin appeared to be quit greedy and she was just the opposite. Magic was still scared from the first heist and here he was

39

talking about hitting stores all the way to Compton this was a plate full. she had enough money right there in her clutches to get what she wanted which was a brand new home for her and Blossom this was the plan sense the power rush seemed to have went to Kevin's head she wondered if backing out now was the right thing to do.

"Can I ask you a question, Kevin?" Magic asks.

"Shoot, baby." Kevin said.

"I thought you said you didn't know no one around here to liquidate the diamond jewelry, and when I went to sleep and wake up I wake up to a stacks of cash staring me in the face, your a sure naught business man aren't you?' Magic asks flipping through the bills trying to count each one.

"Most definitely, tell me did I say something to scare you out of coming with me to New York?" Kevin asks curious.

"No you didn't say nothing to scare me. I just don't think me leaving my cat would be a wise decision after all who would feed her. If Doug's mad at me and I have no family here, and Gee-Gee is tied up with her new man."

"Who's Gee-Gee?" Kevin asks.

"My girlfriend at the club she's harmless she single trying to make a living as a dancer just as I was." Magic explained.

"I feel you but I think it would be wise to sit on the money for a while how would you explain it to everybody whose so use too seeing you broke and struggling?" Kevin asks Magic waiting for a logical answer.

"I'll tell them I hit the lottery." Magic said.

"Yeah right, so if I leave town and come back you're telling me the money will not be spent?" Kevin asks.

"Of course I would spend some of it."

"No, that wouldn't be wise just lay low until I come back." Kevin explained before picking Magic up

40

off the couch and breaking his vow to be strictly business partners he took her up and started to kiss her with one of his sexy wet kisses she melted to his touch.

Meanwhile, Douglas was mad as hell. When he finally reached home still clutching his sweaty palms around the bag he walked miles with, he was steaming in side for the screw up, and would miss Magic with all his heart this was suppose to be the robbery that put them both on top. He wanted to celebrate with her so bad and knew she had to be laid up with Kevin by now. He knew how smooth tongued Kevin was and how he eyeballed Magic the whole time they were working. He could see it and couldn't bear to loose her as a friend and future lover. He planned on telling her how he felt after the heist but things took a drastic turn for the worst. He wonders what she was doing while he stood in the middle of the floor thinking about her. He didn't know nothing about liquidating his diamonds and knew how mad Kevin was at him for smashing the showcase glass. He wanted to just turn everybody in and make amends with his conscious that was eating him up. he knew once he obtained all the cash the diamonds were to bring his way, questions would be asked there was no way a man like him could one day be broke and the next day rich in the hood he lived in. people would definitely ask plenty of questions there was no in and or buts about it. He decided to turn the diamond back over to the store he stole them from or turn them over to the authorities and bring an end to these games he was playing with himself; he dialed the number to the Fulton County Police Department.

Kevin pulled Magic up on her feet pulling her slim body close to his as they melted in each others arms feeling each other like never before this was the one Magic couldn't just let him board that flight to New York with out her by him side. She would just have to take Blossom with her. She refused to let another female dig her French tips in her thugs back not this one he was hers. They made love for hours until James barged in by knocking on Kevin's door. This was the signal to pack up it was time to roll and this was not like Kevin not being ready to "stick and move" like he was taught on the street while hustling "stick and move" James yelled through the door before it opened and he walked in and flopped down on the couch to hear his partners plan.

Kevin told Magic this was her chance to make some real money and run with him all at the same time. He wanted her by his side like Bonnie needed Clyde, and Thelma needed Louise he wasn't willing to let this brown sugar get away it wasn't everyday a thug met his match a female gangsta's they ran scarce this was a sacred union to Kevin.

"Alright I'll go; I'm just going to have to bring my cat with me that's all." Magic said letting Kevin know she was feeling him after he made love to her. She wasn't going to let this strong black man walk out her life never to return.

"I want you to go get your cat and come back in one hour because our flight leaves in two James will not be with us this time, so go handle your business." Kevin announced as he started packing his gear while James helped him.

Magic took a cab home since she left her place in Kevin's Mercedes to hit the jewelry store. She couldn't get home fast enough. She wanted to call Douglas and apologized hoping all was forgiven. She knew Douglas loved the air she breathed and became to jealous over her in front of Kevin in the alleyway.

Magic got out of the cab and broke for the door of her house to call Douglas and tell him about her trip to New York with Kevin. she wanted to thank him for introducing her to him because they hit it off so well she thought Douglas would be happy for her little did she know Douglas had turned the whole crew he put together over to Georgia's finest, and the investigation was under way. Douglas was happy when he walked into the darkness of night carrying a plastic garbage bag full of gold and diamond jewelry and watches to name just a few of the spoils he left the crime scene with. this jealousy that raged deep inside him and the fear of over night success and the stares and looks of his community scared him into a plea for a lesser sentence and a reward for the capture of Magic and Kevin and James, he would turn Magic and the rest of the crew over to the authorities for money but not the money from the heist but the money from the reward from the police.

"Hello Douglas." Magic said into the receiver.

"Oh, Magic how is you?" Douglas said into the phone as him and three of Georgia's finest sat by the phone listening in on the call taping each and every word coming out of Magic's mouth.

"I got some good news Douglas, I'm ok, I just wanted you to know me and Kevin is planning a trip to New York City together can you believe how well we hit it off. He said were going to pull a couple of jobs sorry everything between y'all didn't work out, but I like him and I need the money that's why I feel I need to go."

"Slow down Magic, I'm glad you two hit it off. I sure grabbed a lot of jewelry myself I didn't even notice it until I got home. I was just thinking about what I had done to ruin everything for you and the rest of the crew but I think I grabbed enough to take care of the money I owe and then some." Douglas said.

"Me too and I hope the money is enough to pay off your child support debt. I hope you still have enough to pay for the things you want beyond that like some fly clothes and a little bling." Magic said feeling confident pulling her stacks of cash out of a bag laying them on the table in front of her so she could keep her eye on them before hanging up.

The police pointed to another cop and they made plans to make an arrest but first they had to obtain a search warrant.

Magic's phone rang.

"Hello."

"You're wasting precious time, stick and move." Kevin yelled in the receiver.

"I'm packing now!" Magic said huffing and puffing in the receiver as she threw clothes in a bag and some goodies for her cat Blossom.

She hung up filling the bag with the things she felt she would need once she got to New York City.

Magic loaded up her Audi TT and headed over to Kevin's place hoping she wouldn't make him miss his flight when she pulled up in front of the house she ran around the car up to the front door. She feared not being the one for Kevin like she felt he was the one for her. Indifferences ran rapid in her mind but she ignored each and every one of them.

"Good you made it let's get a move on." Kevin pulled the door closed behind himself and locked it as him and Magic walked to his Mercedes they loaded up her stuff and headed to the airport.

"My man James is going to meet us in the city."

"I'm kind of scares Kevin. I never did nothing like this before shit is moving so fast and I don't want to loose you." Magic explained.

"What do you mean we just pulled a job last night you're a true to the game gangsta now baby? There is no turning back once we enter the Big Apple the big planning session will come into order this is the season to do what we want to as far as robbing jewelry stores are concerned. If you want to live large this is the time to start bringing shit into view. Once we are in just follow my lead I'll teach you everything you need to know to be on top of the game." Kevin explained as they existed the car and walked into the Hartsfield- Jackson Airport of ATL this New York City Thug had his Georgia peach by the hand as she

44

gripped Blossoms cage with a kung fu grip as they ran through the airport. The last call for their flight had been made over the airport intercom. The police burst into Magic's curbside door with such force they knocked it off the hinges while on the other side of town Kevin's house was being invaded. Douglas had been transport to the Fulton County jails with the canteen money he collected as a reward for turning his accomplices in to the police; the deal he had made with the D.A for a lesser sentence had backed fired in his face. He had no idea snitches got ate for breakfast in the County jail and respect was far from being seen. The deal for a lesser sentence was taken back after his back child support dead beat dead report hit the police radio waves and computers.

"Y'all promised me a deal!" he hopped around in his cage with an orange jumpsuit on crying like a bitch after he turned Magic, Kevin, and James deepest dark secrets over the police.

"Just look at it this way you have enough canteen money to last you at least a good year." The cop said as he locked the cell with the electronic hand gadget he held in his hand as he laughed and walked away.

The cop knowing in his mind they were trying to meet a quota and Douglas was just one more sucker down in the eyes of the law. He would be made to work for the state for .50 cent an hour or a dollar if he got lucky.

"Damn, I'm the dumbest nigga I ever known." Douglas said to himself in a whisper as he made up his mattress to lie down and look at the ceiling. He had no one he could call except his mother and she couldn't bail him out of jail from lack of money the one thing that landed him there in the first place.

Magic and Kevin boarded the plane and Blossom went in the back with the other animals.

"I miss my baby." Magic said feeling relaxed in the presence of Kevin as if she had known him for years. She had no idea Douglas had the police over at her house busting the door down ready to make an arrest for the burglary of the Jewelry store. that changed her destiny the conversation had been recorded and the Judge heard it all his command for an arrest started a nation wide search for Magic and Kevin pictures were confiscated from both their residence and posted all across the television screens in Georgia and spreading like the plague from states to state.

Kevin and Magic stepped foot off the plane in LaGuardia Airport in New York City. The crowd was thick and the weather rainy. Kevin saw the police rotating around as if they were looking for something or someone. One ran towards the other as they grabbed their bags off the revolving conveyor belt and walked to the area to collect Blossom, Magic held her cat as Kevin held her by the hand walking as fast as they could towards the exit way of the airport as their hearts raced.

"Damn, where did all those cops come from?" Magic asks looking scared in the eyes.

"I don't know baby, I just know it makes me feel uncomfortable." Kevin said in return.

"Let's get going my boy's are waiting for us to show up." Kevin flagged down a New York City gypsy cab while Magic remains on the side walk waiting for him.

"Come on baby." Kevin said.

Magic and Kevin got in the cab and rode to Brooklyn's Montgomery Street to be exact where the plot for the heist was to take place.

"I know you're kind of nervous but I'm here to tell you we work fast and this will be over before you know it." Kevin explained as the cab drove over the Brooklyn Bridge. The cab came to a sudden stop in front of a large brown stone apartment building.

"Damn it feels good to be back home." Kevin said while taking Magic by the hand guiding her into the building.

"I think New York is dirty and noisy." Magic said expressing her feelings.

"It may be dirty and noisy but it's my home baby and I love it." Kevin replied.

They walked inside the apartment building that smelled like pure urine in the elevator on the way up to the thirteenth floor. Kevin knocked on the door and a light skinned tall dark haired Cuban looking man opened the door. He grabbed Kevin and hugged him tight before he let them both all the way in the house.

"Everyone is here waiting for you man and who's this beautiful woman by your side?" Starsky asks.

"This is my partner from Down Georgia way her name is Magic." Kevin said.

"I love that name." Starsky said.

"Thank you." Magic responded while she's set Blossom free from her cage.

"She's down with the plan, huh." Starsky asks.

All four of Kevin's partners were there waiting for him so they could plan the heist on 47th Street in the Diamond district of New York City.

"What's up man? Come on in here and let's get a move on." Pete said while rolling a blunt emptying the contents in a near by garbage can.

Everybody in the room pulled up a chair and made sure the doors where locked while the planning got under way. Starsky took the floor he was one of the masterminds behind the crew he was good at planning heist. The lights went dim and a projector that sat on the table was turned on a virtual tour of 47th street came across the kitchen wall.

"These guy's really are professionals." Magic whispered in Kevin's ear.

"I would work with nothing less only for you I would as if you did all ready know this." Kevin said speaking of the heist with the unprofessional crew he had just pulled in Georgia while rolling with Douglas.

Meanwhile the streets were already filled with New York's finest they were on the look out for the two Georgia residences whose names were all across each and every television screen and radio station all across America.

"As we all know 47th Street is the Diamond District in New York City this is the largest consumer market for loose diamonds, 90% of the diamond come in by way of New York." Starsky said pointing to the line of stores on the kitchen wall shining through the projector's lens; they planned on taking 47th street by storm that night while the city that never sleep's, slept.

"I hear y'all so when will this go down." Kevin said rubbing both his hands together ready to dig in the pot of gold that waited at the end of his rainbow down on 47th Street.

"Shit, I have no problem with the plan considering." Pete explained as he lit the blunt.

"And why is that, Pete?" Kevin and the other guys ask.

"Shit, that diamond use to be my Great, Great Grandfather's over there in Africa before they stole them and then worked the shit out of my people today to get the shits out the ground. Man all they gave them was bags of rice for all the hard work they did while those mother fuckers are still capitalizing, so let get this shit over and done with so I can kick these damn boots off and relax." Pete said before sitting back down and listening to the serious floor plans that laid before him.

Magic sat there in silence wondering where she would fit in all this since she hadn't a clue to her job function.

"They give bus tours in the diamond district we can get in this way or we can smash some shit and go up in there gangsta style and take what we want." Starsky explained.

"I can see you now shittin in your draws soon as you see a cop car." Pete said as everyone fell on their knees with laughter

"Damn right but I guaranteed you I won't drop not one diamond, man." Starsky explained.

"Alright boys all jokes aside are we going to do this tonight or roll with the tour bus tonight?" Starsky asks with a look of seriousness on his face.

"I rather work at night." everybody answered.

"Yeah me too." Kevin said.

"Me too." Magic said in a soft solemn voice.

"Y'all know April is the beginning of smash and grab season so let take some shit." A voice blurted out sounding immature to Magic's ears.

"They have that smoke cloak machine now man those machine fill the room up with thick smoke which makes it impossible to see what's in front of you; I guess they figure a thief can't steal what he can't see, huh." Pete said as he cracked another joke.

"Who needs to see? Shit I can feel what I want."

Magic and everybody in the room made jokes as they planned the heist that would make them very rich men and women without a care or worry in the world for a long time to come.

"Step one." Pete said as he turned the projector off standing in the front of the room with his arms folded.

"We will be wearing tactic gear it's very necessary." Pete said waiting for a amen.

"Step two; I know this is some scary shit and if you feel you can't handle it back out now." Starsky said while staring Magic down.

"Are you sure your girl is down with this? Because if she can handle it her job will be grabbing all the diamonds she can and once you get them run back to the van and change your tactic gear for your regular clothes." Starsky explained.

"I can handle this." Magic responded scanning the room waiting for one of Kevin's crew to disagree.

"Me and her pulled a job in Georgia and she can handle it." Kevin said vouching for Magic. He wanted her to get all she could while she rolled with him. She needed money so Kevin gave her the chance to make some independently but at the same time protected by him at least that is the hype he sold her.

The time came and Starsky stood by the door handing out tactic gear outfits waiting for all the member's of his crew to put them on and get the necessary tool they would be working with. A bag was passed out to each and every one of them one by one; Magic's heart beat so loud she felt as if it would jump right out her chest.

"You alright baby?" Kevin asks while holding Magic's hand.

"Of course, I can handle this." Magic said while squeezing his.

The truck that was to carry them pulled up to the Montgomery Street apartment door, it was black in color and rough looking. Magic decided she could roll with the best of them like Kevin told her she could. They arrived at the jewelry store in the wee hours in the morning and began swinging and slinging their sledge hammers after the security system had been deactivated in order to enter the first store, Pete was the first one to initiated the first swing once the glass broke

Everyone started grabbing merchandise. Magic was surprised considering this was the same method of B and E Douglas used and Kevin called him America's dumbest criminal what happened to the thug style of doing things or was this it? Magic thought to her self.

"I thought you told me they were professionals with their method of doing things!" She said as she left the scene pissed off as she ran around the corner a man grabbed her arm and pulled her in the alleyway

50

covering her mouth. She looked up and noticed a shiny badge on his jacket and a bunch of cop cars pulled up granting his every command. It was over there was no denying it was over before it really ever started.

"It's over Magic aka Missy Malone from Atlanta Georgia we have your partner Douglas in custody and he told us you would be coming here to the big apple. He also mentioned you were the mastermind behind these heist, cuff her!" The Sergeant yelled.

Kevin looked out the window of the jewelry store and seen cops running from around the corner thick as thieves life had dealt him a faulty blow and his last heist.

"Drop the bag!" The cop yelled as gun fire started to fill the air.

Kevin, Starsky, Pete and the others came out of the store with their pieces in one hand and their bag of diamonds in the other. They refused to lay the guns down or let their bags go. The cops they started firing Kevin was the first one down, one by one they all died laid side by side and across each other on 47th street in front of one of the most prestigious Jewish Jewelry stores on the block. The cop car cruised by as Magic got to say her last good byes on the way to Jail and from there the State Penitentiary. Magic was left alone to face all charges in New York City and in Georgia. Magic received twenty five years to life in both states. When she finish one sentence, if she lives through it she'll be sent to Georgia to live out the other.

*When the chips are down, the way some of us go about getting money is just a root in the tree of evil.

Chapter 3

Counterfeit Life

Gangbanging was all Rakeem knew. All his life he reacted to his environment in a hostile way. He seen them come and go in the hood constantly 1% always made it out if he told the story while the other 99% stayed wishing they could pull the ones that fled the pot of crabs back down into the bucket with them to finish boiling. Education and opportunity was the last thing he expected to come knocking on his door. Like the rich always said money never been a worry to them while all the while it was a constant worry to Rakeem and his peoples. They lived on the lowest totem on the totem pole. They lived in the part of the hood the toughest was scared to sojourn. Like so many others he knew the only way-out of the hood would be if he made it happen. This story takes you into Rakeem's world of gangbanging and the making of counterfeit money. he seen the rich get richer for eighteen years of his life and he prayed for redemption for himself and his family, if it meant falling out of the sky just as long as it came.

The phone rings.

"I got the plates, man!" Darryl said excited standing at the phone booth with his pants hanging past his ass representing his gang's colors of black and gold. He wore his colors no matter what he wore representing to the fullest extent.

"Stop lying, man." Rakeem said sporting the same colors trying to keep up with the latest trends in his style of representing.

"The Mexican got them for me just like he promised; now all we need to do is make the money." Darryl said happier than a fagat in boy's town.

"How in the hell did he get them?" Rakeem asked showing excitement like his gangbanging brother.

"Don't worry about where he got them you just get over here and let's get busy!" Darryl said before hanging up the phone.

"Let's do this!" Rakeem said before bursting out of his mother's front door. The screen practically hung off the hinges. He slammed it shut. His mother yelled to the top of her lungs behind him as he ran down the street Rakeem felt like a god as he walked through his block in the hood of Chicago knowing him and his gangbanging brother was about to make up a batch of counterfeit money. He dreamt of this day for a long time ever since Darryl told him he knew where to get the plates. All the things he wanted to buy and the things he wanted to do was all that seeped through the juices in his mind. He had his share of the hood and wanted to move up and out of there. The gang he rolled with rode around 24/7in stolen cars doing drive by shootings, and arson's were another one of their specialties and killing people for no good apparent reason. He was happy this was coming to a conclusion in his life. Rakeem was ready to live not die a statistic. The daily stares from people who did not know him ate at him constantly as he walked around wearing a invisible shield for protection in front of him, blocking out the stares and judgment replacing them with his hard knock looks and hate towards the enemy. This made him want to project his pain even harder. He would become the blood shedder the hoodlum the cut throat the convict, felon and fugitive, criminal, and devil that some people called him this, on the regular basis.

"Open up, man!" Rakeem yelled through his friend Darryl's door, He beat the door with his fist creating a bunch of noise.

"That you Rakeem, get in here man and look at what we got!" Darryl moved to the side and let his best friends and brother gang banger see what was set up and printing beautiful green $10, $20, $50, and $100's the printer were printing them out like they was on an assembly line. The scanner was hooked up to the printer while the scanner scanned producing beautiful false green bills that looked realistic to the eyes. Money to pay for a new house and cars. Rakeem envisioned the rims spinning as he day dreamt.

"Where did you get the printer that makes this shit look real, man?' Rakeem asks with excitement in his voice. This was the most money he had seen in his whole life.

"If we get caught with this man it's an automactic ten to twenty years, so be careful." Darryl explained. I don't want to go to jail look in his eye as he stood there looking rougher than words.

"That's one chance I'm willing to take." Rakeem said picking up an arm load of the money that was being boxed and taped up.

"These bills will pass through any detector out there.' Darryl said knowing what he was told by the Mexican who sold him the plates.

"Are you so sure of that man? If shit was that easy, how come we haven't been doing this shit along time ago?" Rakeem asked.

"They have ultra violet ray scanners out there man that can tell the difference that's why, man." Darryl explained.

"You been doing your homework haven't you man. I'm glad I put you on. I need intelligence in this operation. "Darryl said while stacking up a fresh batch of hundred dollar bills, nothing was going to

stop his flow, not Rakeem, not his gangbanging
brothers in his gang, and definitely not the police. He
took a hand full of twenties, fifties, and hundreds
shoving them in his pocket for pocket change.

"The rich is getting richer while we're stuck
down here, seems like in the pit of hell. This is it man!
shit is about to take off for us finally. I wish I was
borne an heir to a fortune but I'm not. Brother has to
do what a brother has to do to keep from drowning.
The rich sit up there in that skyscraper plotting
against the poor twenty four seven and I'm tired of it.
Their laughing at us while we're down here doing this
kind of shit to make ends meet. Now their talking
about tearing down our house to build condo's man,
I'll be damn, I'm buying my people a house with my
share of the money." Darryl said while picturing
himself sitting at the wheel in a brand new Cadillac
Escalade truck with spinning rims.

"They think all of us can get out of the ghetto
when in reality some of us can't it's just impossible."
Rakeem expressed as he shoved his pocket full of
bills.

"Yeah…Yeah…Yeah…Rakeem in other words
you're tired of being a roach waiting to get stepped
on." Darryl broke down the feeling his brother gang
banger felt as they boxed up the remainder of the bills
with his favorite presidents staring him pretty in the
face; he kissed the bill and sat it in the box with the
other presidents.

"We are all the way down here on the totem
pole of life man." Rakeem rattled on with his mouth
talking about financial status as if he knew what it
really took to make ends meet.

"All I can tell you man is get over it and spend
very wisely because after tonight there is no telling
when we'll be able to make any more money." Darryl
as he gathered up the evidence that laid around.

"Shit... from the looks of this we'll be climbing that ladder real soon." Rakeem said counting his pocket change.

"The sky's the limit man like scare face, can't you see that!" Darryl said trying to wake Rakeem's mind up to reality.

"I guess your right man because there is no way I'm letting this deal slip through my hands." Rakeem responded.

"Let me explained this to you man each bill have a water mark on them when held up to the light that's why we used water proof ink." Darryl explained.

"What are you telling me this for it's not like I can make some money by myself without you, man." Rakeem said letting Darryl know he was to be trusted.

"And one other thing man most of these fake bills look realistic enough to pass through the bank of your choosing." Darryl explained as he watched his buddy's reaction.

"For real man? Rakeem said as he plotted in his mind what he planned on doing with his share of the money.

"To be honest I want to take mine to the bank too." Darryl said plotting as he talked.

The two worked over time boxing up money and counting this was like a dream come true sitting in a room surrounded by money like Scare face or the God- Father this made the two men day dream the room became silent.

It took half the night before they finished.

"This here is my share and this is yours I wouldn't spend it right away either man bury it somewhere until I give you the green light." Darryl said as he loaded up the rented u-haul truck taking the money to its final resting place.

Darryl took his money to his mother's house making the place hotter than it already was he buried half of it in the back yard. He planned on laying low for a while because once the money started floating the heat would be on from the popo and revel gang bangers including his own gang. Rakeem was ignorant to the counterfeiting game he had no idea he had just walked into his own death sentence.

The following morning he left the house to hook up with his home boy Darryl. They knew each other seemed like forever since child hood. In a sense they were like blood brothers belonging to the same gang and all Darryl needed to know could they actually pass the money through the bank without getting busted. This is what laid dormant in his mind he needed to know and Rakeem would be the guinea pig to prove the theory if his theory proved to be genius he knew he would be one rich nigga on the run. He would sacrifice to gain the riches that laid at the end of this long hard road that he traveled in his nineteen years in life. His gang was his life but when it all boiled down his gang wouldn't be there when his family needed money to pay the light bill and where was his gang when the fridge was empty. Darryl fell back on his bed and grabbed his headphones cutting the music up extra loud listening to one of his favorite gangsta this made him feel like a true bonified gangsta. Darryl figured he could beat the system like so many other's before him that had travel down the same road as he. Like Bonnie before she hooked up with Clyde. and the other television movie that played in his head while listening to his music the pictures played so fast he couldn't keep up so finally he gave up the thought until Rakeem's face came into view he planned on coaxing his life long best friend into taking his share of the counterfeit money to the Chicago National Bank one of the biggest branches in Chicago and cash his share in for the real dead presidents. He never once considered the real problem that laid ahead the real family that held the key's to his soul his gang and his leader T.J. he feared T. J. to a certain extent he knew if he messed with T. J. his whole world could come crashing down in a matter of minutes. The Chicago streets had been ran by T. J. and his blood gang brother's for a long time and making money was one of their fortes they lived, ate and breathed money. So time became an important factor. Who ever made money on the streets of Chicago wearing Black and Gold was obligated to report all dividends to the family no one could hide the fact and Darryl knew this but still took a chance.

Rakeem took his counterfeit money to his mother's house putting each and everyone in the house in danger but really not caring. He took his duffle bag and threw it on his twin bed all the while day dreaming about the pretty light skinned babe he wanted to take out for a while but never had the cash to so this had been on his mind for a while now he had been wanting her for month and this money would give him leverage. This would make him a true to life gangster like he always' wanted to be. Rakeem daydreamed until the phone rang making him pop from under his own spell.

"Don't spend the money right away because if we get caught this could get us in a world of trouble." His heart jumped just thinking about it over and over again like a broken record.

"Rakeem!" the voice blurted out of the receiver scaring him even more.

"Yeah...man." Rakeem answered be led by a power stronger than his own.

"Did you spend any yet?" Darryl asked control the situation.

"Didn't you tell me not to spend none man?" Rakeem answered.

"Good!" Darryl said in response before laying the floor plans on him.

"I want us to go to the bank tomorrow and put what we talked about yesterday into affect." Darryl said still strolled across his bed.

"I thought you told me not to mess with the money until shit melted on the street at least that is the impression you left me believing." Rakeem said trying to think for himself for the first time in his life.

"That's alright man the plans have changed I gave it a lot of thought and I want to do this, and remember don't tell the other brother's about this. This is my project those nigga's can't be down with this. Do you think they cared when my mother light got cut off so I advise you Rakeem to listen to each and every word coming out my mouth as if this was the last word, tomorrow we are going to take the money to the bank bring at least twenty gran with you in a brief case. Do you have a brief case nigga? And wear a suit I know you got a suit in there some where." Darryl said feeling Rakeem out.

Rakeem stood there listening like he was in a hypnotic state that he couldn't pull himself from under.

"Ok... man." Was all that came out of Rakeem's mouth?

"You know how our gang operate so please don't tell no one in the gang about this if they find out we could end up marked for death. I changed my mind about buying a house here and I think it would be wise to get the hell out of town." Darryl said still feeling Raceme out to see how intelligent he really was.

"Man... where in the hell will we go?" Raceme asks not understanding the danger he would be in once he obtained all the money and his gang got wind of it.

"I don't know about you man but I'm going to ATL or South Carolina down there on Myrtle Beach where I have family none of those nagger's better come down there looking for me because believe me cuss they won't find me." Darryl said letting his plans out the bag.

"How about T. J. do you think he'll just let you walk away especially after he finds out you moved up in the world without promoting the family too?" Raceme asks.

Darryl was shocked to hear such an intelligent question rolling off his partners lips. He knew he had some more planning to do in order to stay one step ahead of the game.

"Are you sure this thing with the bank is going to work, man?" Raceme asked with concern in his voice. He had no idea of how the banking system was run he just knew the streets in which he dwelled. He let Darryl set all the rules as he just followed his lead.

"I tell you what, Raceme sleep on it man, and hit me back tomorrow." Darryl said before hanging up on his friend for life.

T. J. passed through all the ranks of gang life he was at the top. His following had moved him all the way up to Supreme Crown Authority. He had been to prison on numerous occasions. He ran shit in and out of the facility. T. He's word was like gold to them who wore his colors on their backs if they didn't follow his orders and do what was expected of them the streets could turn-on them as fast as a bullet came out of a guns chamber. Just the mention of T. J.; s name sent chills up and down Raceme's spine he knew T. J. was there for him when he needed to belong to a clique he opened his doors up and let him in his growing family. He knew how in the streets secrets traveled from tongue to tongue and this was one secret he hoped didn't reach T. J. 's ears. Especially since he had the North side and the South side on lock down everything seemed to pass through T. J.; s ears first. T. J. got word that some fake money was about to hit the block and he put his crew on look out detail, T. J. had all the gadget to detect and decode no matter what the occasion called for and his other special knack for maneuvering his crews like the military.

"I wonder whose floating all the fake bills on the block?" T. J. asked one of his soldiers.

He hunched his shoulders.

Just hope it ain't any of mine. I don't know how I'd act if one of y'all brought me some fake bills for some of my product." T. J. said as he took a deep pull of his blunt.

"I can find out for you. I have a couple of snitches out there on the streets." T. J. 's lieutenant answered.

"Find out if it's the shorties, or the ECB's, I know it can't be the nation, or Loco's, or the so lidos or the Queens they can't be floating no money." T. J. said as he laid back in the seat of his convertible choking off a mega pull the Cush weed that he woke up to everyday before he brushed his teeth weed, graffiti, shootings, narcotics, stabbings, beatings, weapons, extortion, assaults, intimidation., was the rode to riches to T. J. he loved the fact that he could co- create fear into his victims without even trying society feared him and he knew it. This is the life he chose over anything else. He found that when he used fear like a spoiled child he could move things once this point was established like a birth right all else would fall into play.

"I want to know who got the plates because if this kind of money is floating around it could end up in my stash and we can't have that with the cops wanting to shut shit down I paid them off to well for that shit!" T. J. explained to his side kicks that surround him on a daily basis he tried to convert his new comers into believing he could protect them from anything in life or in this world including the police. T.J. wore his tattoos proudly on his wrist the most painful place there is to get tattooed. he displayed the pain he been through in life on his vital parts of his body on his lower back he wore a five point star and on his side torso ALKN and a pitch fork was visible for all eyes to see. He represented his gang the best way he knew how and if all the above wasn't proof enough then so be it.

61

"I will die for you." Are the words that sprayed out of his mouth when he stood up making his rounds like a C. O in a prison yard. All his crews' eyes were on him as if he could resurrect the dead.

"Bring me the balls of those nigga making fake bills. I will heavenly compensate the one who does." T. J. said before walking out of the door with his queen by law by his side. He stepped up in his brand new black hummer with the gold spinning rims and trims and pulled off with his favorite rap blurting out of the speakers not caring about the law.

Darryl planned all night him and his home boy would be going to the bank the following morning. He would give instruction while sitting in the wings to see the outcome of his plan once the sun came up in the East him and Rakeem would be hitting up Chicago National bank. The morning quickly came he called Rakeem to wake him up but first he wanted to walk to the corner store to get a box of fruit loops for breakfast and a pint of milk. All the while testing out the money on the Arabs that owned the store he figured a store this size definitely wouldn't have no kinds

Of detectors to scan the fake bills if luck was on his side the Arab would just hold the money up to the light. Darryl was sure his money would pass the test. Darryl walked into the store and put his morning breakfast on the counter. He looked into Ali's eyes before handing him the counterfeit twenty; the word was on the street T. J.'s crew wouldn't stop until they brought him exactly what he wanted which were the balls of the counterfeiter or counterfeiter's.

The North side was hot as well as the Southside. The Arab that owned the store paid his dues on the regular for protection from T. J. and his crew.

"Good morning." Ali said before Darryl handed him the twenty he remembered seeing Darryl standing on the corner on numerous occasions wearing black and gold representing his crew but the Arab could tell something was different about Darryl this morning.

"Give me my change in singles." Darryl demanded in a hard voice.

The Arab held the money up to the light then he reached under the counter and pulled out a yellow marker marking the money, Darryl bucked for the front door trying to make break for it for he knew his plan to pull the wool over the Arabs eyes didn't work.

"What are you doing man?" Darryl yelled before grabbing the bag off the counter. He made a straight shot through the door and the Arab wasn't far behind. He had the counterfeit twenty in hand and his .32 in the other hand.

The Arab yelled down the block of Dearborn Street and all became silent the gun went off so fast there was no time to duck the bullet that sped out the chamber. The bullet landed in Darryl's killing him instantly. The scene became noisy with police cars screeching their tires while coming to a stop drawing their weapons on sight. Chicago PD made it impossible to move around from point A to point B. there so many of them from the forensic crew to the investigators. Rakeem woke up on the right side of the bed that morning he felt optimistic about what the day held for him and his life long gangbanging Brother Darryl. He knew if things went right he would no longer represent his gang by wearing their colors or by doing anything gang related things were looking good the only thing that held him back was the fact the money had to be converted into the real thing. He built up his confidence hoping the plan to wear a suit with brief case in hand would work.

He wore the suit his mother gave him hoping he would graduate from high school before he dropped out. He slipped on the slacks before looking into the mirror at his silhouette. He like it he looked like a Wall Street tycoon he took a old briefcase filling it up with fake twenty, tens, fifties, and hundreds, his stomach filled with butterfly's as he stood over it. He put on a fake invisible shield that had protected him so many times before from the

Elements in gang fights, drive by's or what ever violent acts him and his brother gang banger were involved in. He wanted to leave this lifestyle behind him, becoming disenchanted with the hard knock life and the gang life style of teaching. All the killing he committed at such an early age, not to mention the robbery he committed just last week this life filled with mayhem and misshapes was getting out of control. Rakeem had no idea what was going on in Darryl's neighborhood. Darryl was supposed to meet him at the bank to cash in the money. He hadn't a clue which teller he would approach to ask for help if Darryl didn't show up and do his part like he was supposed too. He stopped at the front door of the bank trying to pull himself together mind, body, and soul. He waited patiently for his cue to make his move but Darryl wasn't in sight. the master mind didn't show up he looked for the u-haul truck to pull up at any moment but it never did, So Rakeem thought quick and approached the first black teller he seen. She had a serious soft look about her as Rakeem walked up to the window looking more professional then he ever did in his whole life. The teller sat there counting a hand filled with twenty and hundreds she counted so fast Rakeem could not keep up her hands where moving so fast.

"May I help you, sir?" the teller asks with a smile on her face.

"As a matter of fact you can." Rakeem answered straightening his tie.

Rakeem put his briefcase on the counter turning it in the direction of the teller; she smiled before asking another question.

"And your name, sir?" the teller asks.

"I did tell you my name didn't I?" Rakeem asked.

"No you didn't, sir." The teller said becoming agitated.

Rakeem looked over his shoulders one last time to see if Darryl had walked into the bank unbeknown to him while he was gaining the tellers confidence.

"My name is Darryl Taylor." Rakeem said with a smile on his face not knowing Darryl's fate.

"Alright Mr. Taylor what exactly did you want me to do with all this cash, do you want to open an account or do you already have one with us? How about a safety deposit box or a checking account we here at Chicago national want to assist you in your banking needs anyway we can, Mr. Taylor." The teller said sounding like a commercial.

"I want to." Rakeem said before catching himself.

"You want to what, Mr. Taylor." The teller asks looking at Rakeem as if he was crazy.

"I want to know if you could do this for me. I know we just met but I really need a favor." Rakeem asks practically begging.

"That's my job to assist you Mr. Taylor the best way I can so please tell me exactly what it is you need and I'll see what I can do for you." The teller disclosed.

"By the way what's your name, ma'am?" Rakeem asks standing there nervous and shaking underneath his skins.

"April." The teller said.

"Well...April I will give you a thousand dollars if you will change this money into fresh crisp bills for me." April hunched her shoulders for she was unfamiliar with this procedure this was like bank robbery to her because it wasn't in the employee handbook and that's what she knew the procedure too. So she did what she thought was right by turning Rakeem over to a higher authority the head teller.

"What do you mean you will give me a thousand dollars to turn this money into new money for you? April asks demanding to find out the answer.

"This money I have here in this brief case is old money and I want to trade it in for new bills." Rakeem explained.

"Now, why didn't you say so but first I will have to take you in the back so you can open up an account?" April explained trying to cover herself.

Rakeem fed April, Darryl's information from his birth date to his high school to put in her computer. He hated Darryl for not showing up at the bank like he was suppose too in the first place. But little did he know Darryl was dead shot and killed by a flying bullet that landed in his back for trying to past off the counterfeit bills to an Arab. The teller called Rakeem to the back of the bank to a room where he would have to wait his turn to open an account he sat there nervous and jittery.

"They'll be with you in a minute." April said as she closed the door behind her.

"Excuse me... who will be with me?" Rakeem asks before the door closed completely. He wondered why she wouldn't take care of the business herself for the cool quick thousand he offered her.

"The head teller will be with you sir and the answer to the question you ask me is no I don't want to loose my job for the thousand dollars you offered me" April said before closing the door tightly behind her.

"Hello... Mr. Taylor." The head teller said when she opened the office door looking like an FBI officer.

She guided Rakeem to step into her office.

"So you want to open an account with Chicago National Bank exactly how much money are you planning on depositing with us today. The head teller asks as she sat down with her eyes on Rakeem the whole time.

"I want to... umm." Rakeem stuttered scared to talk the ghetto came out of him at that moment he didn't and wouldn't turn in his brother not by a long shot especially if he didn't want to get shot.

He wanted to dash for the door but something was holding him back he held on to his brief case so tight he didn't want to let it go.

"I tell you what if you decide you want to open an account today I will charge you five dollars a month how about it Mr. Taylor? So just give me all your information so I can feed it into our computer system." This made Rakeem extremely nervous he almost pissed his pants.

"My name is Darryl Taylor and I live on the North side of Chicago." Rakeem said lying through his teeth while all the while still clutching his briefcase.

The teller reached for the briefcase so she could count the content that laid within she saw twenty, tens, fifties, and hundreds all stacked up nicely ready to be transacted into fresh green real bills.

"Excuse me Mr. Taylor." The teller said before getting up from her desk while reaching for the briefcase to take to the head of the bank.

Rakeem sat there still in a comatose state. Not knowing what the outcome of his backwards move would bring. He sat there twirling his thumbs contemplating his next move. He wanted to run but he remembered his gangbanging brother told him the money was good enough to pass through the banking system he went on a gut feeling to remain seated and wait for the head teller to come back with his briefcase filled with the one and only thing that would help him get out of the gangbanging lifestyle. The money was supposed to be so realistic it could pass through any detector at least that is what he was told. All security devices were supposed to be null in void this made Rakeem confident. The teller made a move to a thick wooden door this is when he became extremely nervous. The teller had all of Darryl's information if any one was to fall it was going to be him. Rakeem thought as he sat there scared to move as if invisible hand held him bound.

The big thick wooden door opened as the head teller and the banks president stepped outside of it before closing the door behind them.

"Hello." The banks president said.

Rakeem spoke back in return.

"Mr. Taylor is it? I just want to be the first person to tell you you're under an arrest." The president said before Rakeem jumped out his seat. And bucked for the door as the door flew open Chicago's finest was standing there ready to make an arrest they threw him on the floor so hard they cracked his tooth.

"I'm not the one you want!" Rakeem screamed as they hand cuffed him.

"If you're not the one then who is?" the cop asks with concern in his voice.

"He got the plates from a Mexican." Rakeem explained trying to get set free.

The cops didn't want to hear no more, Rakeem knew this was the only way out of the gang that held him back for so many years and ruined his life he knew once T. J. found out about the counterfeit money he would eventually come after him and Darryl as the police stuffed him in the car he could hear T.J in his head making one of his popular speeches as the car door slammed in his face.

(The speech)

"I'm the leader of this crew and if you want to be down you will steal cars, sell dope, brutalize and rob people even the elderly for me if that's what I want you to do and no one else. If you and your families are to live in this neighborhood in Chicago as you know I run the North side and the South side of Dearborn Street in other word Chicago streets are mine. I will give you an identity and discipline you the way I see fit because your mother's obviously didn't do their jobs with you recognition you will only get this from me." This is the first speech that popped into Rakeem's mind as the police cruiser cruised down the streets showing him familiar scenes as it past the spot and a variety of other post Rakeem reminisced.

(The speech continues)

"Love verses money. Your love will be to further our reputation on the streets and as far as the money goes it will be beyond your reach. You'll have to go through me to make money do you understand." T.J. said in the movie in Rakeem's head. all of these thoughts and speeches came into view Rakeem knew this was it there was no getting out no matter how bad he wanted it. When the story hit the streets he would be called another brother down no matter how him and Darryl tried to reach beyond there normal sphere by making counterfeit money the man wanted him and they finally had him in their clutches. As he sat there quiet the cop turned around and announced.

"We just scraped a young black male off the side walk for trying to pass off some counterfeit money down there at one of those corner stores as a matter of fact the young man just so happened to have the same name as you Darryl Taylor. Rakeem feared going to prison he knew once he got inside he would be killed by one of T. J.'s crew before this could happen he made the quick decision to take his own life. As soon as the cop car pulled into the sally port Rakeem came up with a plan he knew the officer would disarm himself before taking him inside, Rakeem kicked the partition between himself and the police officers he wouldn't stop even when ordered too. The officer stepped out of the car throwing him the ground.

"These cuffs are killing me officer that's why I was going off back there!" Rakeem said coaxing the officer to loosen them up.

The officer told him to assume the position so he could loosen the cuffs just when he opened the lock on his hand cuff Rakeem grabbed the officer's revolver putting it to his head. When the officer went to grab it back Rakeem pulled the trigger ending his life. Blood splashed all over the officers faces the head officer stood there in shock for the unfortunate accident. He never seen a suicide up close and personal this would change that officers life forever and changed a planned chapter in Rakeem's fate his reign had come to a destructive and horrible end. Rakeem couldn't see himself left alone to fin for himself in a prison system ran by gang bangers where murders and killings happened everyday behind the walls of the concrete jungle neither did he know his death wouldn't change the construction and the illegal movement of his mother from her home for the construction of condo's for the rich.

Chapter 4

Catch Me If You Can

The prison gates opened as Keisha stepped out her release date finally was approved after time after time being turned down ten years. The female judge handed her five years ago. When she stood in front of her highly addicted to crack. She thought she would never get out. As Keisha walked outside the gate her ex-room mate Danice waited in her car patiently.

"Sweet Freedom!" Keisha screamed as she reached for the handle of the fire red Jaguar.

"Damn girl I didn't think those stiff shirts would ever let you out of that shit hole!" Danice yelled sitting at the driver's wheel looking fresher than ever.

"Look at you. Wow you look rich. Danice what have you been doing since you got out?" Keisha asks waiting for an answer to her question.

Danice stayed fresh she wore the newest urban styles to go with her personality and lifestyle. She been a true gangsta bitch all her life down for the count on numerous occasions and she didn't care if she went down again. She was tough enough to handle it

Danice motto was "catch me if you can" she knew how to make an entrance where ever she went to clubs or in prison where ever the winds blew her. She lived her life as a fearless sista, spending fifteen years behind bars in the Virginia State Prison system a common wealth bible buckle state working for fifty cent an hour in the prison laundry was all she knew beyond her call of duty.

"I been living that's what I been doing baby girl, since I step foot out of that slave camp trying to kill time until you my woman got out. What you think I been doing?" Danice said feeling on her girls' leg trying to rekindle old feelings.

"So what your telling me is you haven't been having sex since you been home with males or females? Keisha asks.

"Kill all those questions. Aren't you just glad to be out of there?" Danice asks as she yelled out of her Jaguar window to the white corrections officer she screamed obscenities and stuck her middle finger up for all to see as she pulled off leaving dust circulating in the air and skid marks on the ground.

"I have to find a job and report to a probation and parole officer so for real for real I'm not free until that part of my life is over." Keisha said as she sat there looking bohemian from head to toe with her long red dreds hanging down her back, the same outfit she wore in prison was the outfit she wore when she stepped out if prison.

"Fuck a PO I'm going to Cali and I want you with me. I have a couple of things lined up there so I'll be taking care of you from now on." Danice said as she stopped the Jag and reached over kissing her woman on the lips.

Danice remembered deep in her mind the many night she and Keisha made love after lights out and their cell door was locked. As they kissed Danice couldn't contain herself it had been years since she felt a woman's touch especially one who had been on the inside who knew how to treat a woman.

"Damn I missed you Keisha you just don't know how I yearned for your touch, let's get you some fresh gear before we head to my place. Danice said anticipating Keisha touch.

"You never answered my question? Where did you get the money to buy yourself a Jaguar? Shoot some people never get on their feet when they get out and here you go driving a top of the line Jag." Keisha said looking serious as a heart attack.

"Baby, you ain't seen nothing yet, I been pulling jobs here and there that's how I came across this car once I get you established I have a couple of friends I want you to meet." Danice said.

"I knew it you been playing on me haven't you? Keisha asked as she turned around in her seat raising her voice acting ghetto and out of zinc.

"Calm down you sound like a brained washed fool listen up if you want to continue to roll with me your going to have to pull yourself together because the shit I'm into now pays the bills and then some you know I love to dress and eat good, not to mention I love you and I want to take care of you Keisha. So all I'm asking is that you leave the jealousy behind at Goochland prison where it belongs. I have no room for that kind of behavior in my life your going to have to have a tight mental to be with me." Danice explained.

"Who are the people you want me to meet, Danice?" Keisha asks as they pulled into the local mall they sat in the car in deep conversation before going shopping for some brand new rags.

"I don't think this is a good time to share that information in time in time, baby." Danice took a deep breathe she knew she had her hands full with Keisha reentering her life not knowing who she became since she was released three years ago she changed.

"Do I know these people you're talking about?" Keisha asks as if she been in Danice life forever.

"I'm here for you. I don't see any of your family members here trying to help you get back on your feet as you can see I'm real. I have nobody else to help me either." Danice said.

Danice bought Keisha all the clothes her heart desired and shoes to match. she took Keisha to get her dreds tightened and her nails done by the time they finished shopping the back seat and the trunk of the Jag was filled with packages from the gap, Victoria secrets, Dillard's and a wide variety of other famous designer stores, Danice never once complained about running out of money.

"Damn, where did you get all the money from you been home for three years and your spending like there's no tomorrow?" Keisha asks curious if there was illegal activity going on.

"And if I was. Why does it matter so much to you?" Danice asks.

"Because I'm your girl remember." Keisha said.

"I want to be real with you because we been through too much shit together remember in Goochland prison when we whipped those white girls' asses and took their canteen." Danice said as she turned down a long dark road and drove up a steep hill.

"Yeah, I remember that and remember when they closed the whole prison down because some chick came in with TB they locked us down for two long weeks." Keisha said reminiscing and wondering why they were driving down the long dark road she looked around for a sign of life to find none.

"How could I forget that, that was the two weeks I spent turning you out. Remember?" Danice said as she parked her Jag in the two car garage.

"Wow, whose house is this your mother's?" Keisha asks.

"No, this is my house." Danice answered with confidence in her voice.

The huge brick brownstone was beautiful beside the two car garage it had double doors and ocean in the back yard Keisha could hear the waves crashing against the rocks as they lugged all her packages inside the house. Danice made sure Keisha was extremely comfortable offering her drinks, food and a place to lay down if choose too.

"You're going to have to tell me how to get one of these." Keisha said as she looked at Danice's house with all the Ralph Lauren décor that surrounded them from the lamps to the wall paper and couch navy blue and white was the color décor.

"What's mine is yours baby, each and everything I did and do is for you. I knew when you came home you would be needing a place to crash so I had to do what I had to do to get all this." As Danice was about to tell Keisha what she did for a living her phone begin to ring.

Keisha sat down at the kitchen table acting as if she wasn't listening in on Danice's call.

"Solomon what's up, man?" Danice said when she answered.

Keisha became immediately jealous, Danice left the room walking through her big living room passing all her beautiful furniture she pushed the door open to an office that adjoined, inside her office where four computers sat. Keisha followed. Her eyes were scanning the room wondering how could Danice afford her new high maintenance lifestyle because in prison she didn't have a pot to piss in. She figured what ever she was into worked because she lived a life of extreme wealth now like they said there is light after the light.

Danice finished her conversation with her gentleman caller Solomon. she sat at her computer desk and called Keisha over to her grabbed both Keisha's hands ready to break the news of how things begin to look up for her and she wanted her to be down with her in her life of crime and her new calling.

"Baby, I love you and I wouldn't dare bring you into harms way. But since I been home I had to do something's I'm not particularly proud of. I did my time for the petty crimes I use to do and now I'm involved in a ring." Keisha got down on her knees in between Danice's legs listening to the story she was about to create to get her to believe the dream she was living.

"I met this man he's from Nigeria Africa and his name is Solomon." Danice said.

"Did you screw him?" Keisha said asking the only question she was taught to ask in any given situation.

"Get your mind out the gutter and listen to me please." Danice phone rang but she ignored it this moment was extremely important to her life and her love life and her future.

"I'm not even going to answer that question because it's crazy, Solomon introduced me to a new way of life. Keisha the things he taught me will carry us through no matter where we decide to go, I just want to get out of Virginia. I just might end up back in jail and I don't want that, the job Solomon taught me gets me quick cash in large quantities and I can work from home in my own office, listen baby I can rob a bank right here in the privacy of my own home. There no security guards, no police, and no camera's this is our ticket to true freedom since the man won't give it to us." Danice hoped deep in her heart that Keisha would want to be down and continue to roll with her, because if she didn't now that the cat was out the bag she would be have to be put to sleep she wasn't willing to let her walk out the door carrying such valuable information.

"I'm on papers baby and you know this. I made it clear to you when you picked me up as a matter of fact this was the first thing that came out of my mouth." Keisha said scared of going back to prison.

Danice became violently loud.

"Didn't I tell you fuck your P.O .you don't need those motherfuckers Keisha if I teach you what I know you'll be truly free and they won't touch you, you'll be untouchable." Danice yelled.

"How would all this work Danice you just slapped me in the face with all this how did you expect a sista to react?" Keisha screamed back.

"First of all let's both calm down, come here." Danice grabbed her woman and grind her body close to hers while she kissed her passionately on the lips.

"Damn I missed you while you were gone it's been very lonely" Danice said as she took her woman by the hand leading her upstairs into a large bathroom where her Jacuzzi was heated and ready for two she peeled Keisha's clothing off and hers just the same they both lowered their bodies into the heated hole in the floor adding muse to the fire.

"I want you." Danice said as she grabbed Keisha like she was a man tonguing her into submission. They both moaned as they made love melting into each others arms, when they stepped out of the Jacuzzi Keisha started out asking more questions. She became increasingly more curious, Danice knew once she finished making love to her woman for old time's sake she would and could bring her around to her way of thinking.

"What would my position be if I decided to roll with you on this?" Keisha asks standing there naked drying her dreads with her Pepsi cola bottle shape.

"I can show you better than I could tell you."

"How?" Keishe asks still thinking about how good Danice had did it to her and still feeling the affects.

"I became some what of a computer geek while you been gone, my jobs are to send out e-mails to victims of circumstance. in other words I have to find people who have brand new computers and people who are not hip to the game, then once I reel them in I'll get all the information I can from them, like their names, socials, date of birth, and all the other info they are willing to share online you see they are the ones who paid for my Jaguar, this house, and me and your clothes, so do you want to be down Keisha because I really need you,"Danice said.

Keisha needed Danice just as bad as she needed her especially after being release with twenty five dollars and a bus ticket, she knew society wasn't about to let her get her life back, they would rather keep her down so the C.O.'s that ruled over her twenty four seven could stay employed, not to mention the judges that were ready to throw the book at each and every black face that stood in front of them, she felt like there was no true justice in the justice system, before she went down again at least if she rolled with Danice she would get to enjoy life a little before they caught up with her again.

"I'm down count me in." Keisha said with a distant look in her eye.

"Good I knew you'd come around." Danice was happy she grabbed Keisha around the waist picking her up.

"So will I be doing the same thing your doing?" Keisha asks.

"I don't know yet Solomon is the boss of the whole operation. I will let him and the others know about you and from that point he'll set you up with a job." Danice said.

Danice and Keisha made love all night and the next morning there was a loud thump at the front door.

"Danice someone's banging at your door." Keisha whispered shaking Danice so she'd wake up.

Danice got up slipping on her robe when she opened the door Solomon, Victor, and their other associates walked in.

"What's up Solomon?" Danice asks wiping the cold from the corner of her eyes.

"I heard you have company." Solomon said as he looked around trying to find out who Danice company was his ring was a tight clique that knew everything about its members Solomon wasn't about to let a stranger show up and spoil everything.

"My woman was released yesterday she's staying here with me. I planned on calling you this morning but I see somebody beat me to the punch." Danice said.

"Where is she, is she on papers?" the flow of questions came so fast Danice couldn't answer them all, the 6'1 African wearing a beige linen Armani suit walked around until he found what He was looking for he ran up to Danice bed room standing over Keisha as she laid their in comfort.

"Hi." Keisha said as she laid there in shock wondering who this man was.

"Hello, I'm Solomon, what's your name?"

"Keisha." She pulled the covers up over her chin trying to hide her face.

"Keisha he's my boss." Danice said as she plopped down on the edge of the bed.

"So you just came home and I hear you want a job is you on papers?" Solomon asks.

"I'm not on papers and yes I need a job." Keisha said hoping to gain his confidence.

"Good if what you say is true because we don't need no P.O.'s snooping around here if you want to work for me I would suggest you get up get dress and meet me down stairs." Solomon said as he walked out the bedroom and back downstairs to the office the meeting was to take place. Solomon stood up telling all his followers they would be graduating to another level he explained that they were about to start hitting up Corporations because the little man was not paying enough, him and his ring had just about drained peoples bank accounts from state to state for far too long, he felt as if he was untouchable like so many foreign gangsters, he never once regretted hitting Americans up for their cash he felt they owed him for what had happened to so many of his people generations ago, he felt Americans didn't care about no one but themselves in a selfish manner, only a handful cared about anybody other then themselves, he hated the man for coming to his country destroying lives and breaking up families for their own selfish gain and he felt he should give them a taste of their own medicine. he knew in order to be here in such a rich country he would have to capitalize. He liked shopping at the finest stores, driving top of the line cars from Bentley's to riding in limo's and eating lobster and king crab to the fill. while riding the waves in his expensive yacht this was a gamble worth taking if caught he would be shipped back to Nigeria that was the beauty of it all and it was called diplomatic Immunity, Solomon refused to work as a domestic for no one he wanted revenge for his ancestor and would do what ever to get what he wanted, payback was a bitch but somebody had to do it.

"We will not work slowly now we have to invade and take what we want just like the man did when they took people from my land turning them into domestic's slaves, generation after generation nothing have change except everything's become more glamorous and like idiots people still believe the hype. Commercialization. The room was completely silent his way of teaching was like a Sunday sermon to Danice and to his new follower Keisha they both became victims to his way of teaching the words that came out of his mouth made sense to them especially the facts about slavery, both their minds flashed back to the prison as he continued to speak Keisha and Danice thought about how the C.O.'s forced them to do jobs they didn't want to do in the heat in the summer without air conditioners and a freezing laundry in the winter washing tons and tons of dirty and bloody and shitty laundry for only fifty cents an hour for ten hours to fifteen hours a day. the facts that even when a prisoner was sick they had to work or if they threw their back out they had to work this made them want the illusion that Solomon caste even more they both believed each and every word coming out of his mouth as if he was a great prophet who wanted vengeance and came to America to reap it. Keisha envisioned herself in fly African gauze as he talked she had converted her whole American existence to that of Nigerian Decent.

"He's right Danice this makes me want to be down even more." Keisha said believing his illusions whether fact or fiction.

"The first move will be to become Corporate Coffers ladies and get rich quick." Solomon said as his associates sat there quite acting like trained professionals thieves.

"We are going to reel it all in from Corporations big checks for millions of dollars, why should we steal $5,000 or even $ 50,000 when we can reel in $ 500,000 or more where going for the gusto." Solomon's law was casted and a plan created.

Danice and Keisha's mouths fell open all they seen in their mind where dollar signs.

"The checks will be written by the companies and stolen by us Danice your job will be to come up with the phony addresses, Keisha you'll be responsible for getting the postal boxes Victor will get the identification we'll be needing since he's our inside man, I'll open the brokerage accounts needed and the other loose ends will be handled by me.

Keisha shook her head yes this was the financial miracle she been waiting for especially if all the information that came out of Solomon's mouth was true she got a rush just from listening a rush better than a dope high.

"Suppose we get caught!' Keisha asks looking more naïve to the game than ever.

All eyes turned in her direction, Solomon laughed at how naïve she was.

"They didn't get stopped kidnapping my people from their lands so what's a piece of paper with six digits on it that small and unnoticeable." Solomon said.

"Everything will go smoothly Keisha I promise." Danice said trusting Solomon methods.

"Once we get the checks they'll be cashed immediately and the money transferred out the

country after that you'll both receive your shares."
Victor said.

"Damn he's smart." Keisha said as she walked
towards Solomon to shake his hand, he was a savior
in her desperate eyes at the time when she needed
saving most.

"Keisha your new identity will be Delores Gains
and always dress professional like you work in a
corporate setting when your doing your job, I barely
know you but I'm trusting since you're a friend of
Danice's your alright. Solomon said.

"No problem I'll dress professional." Keisha
said lying to herself if Solomon knew she was on
papers he would had never let her in his world, Keisha
knew she was told she had forty eight hours to report
but she just ignored the rules of the common wealth
state, she pushed the fear out of her mind and went
along with Solomon's plan. Warrants written up if she
didn't show her face to her P.O office by day break.

Solomon and his boys left Danice in charge of
Keisha's human reactions to the plan. she knew how
dangerous the African's she worked for could get if the
orders where not followed, Danice paced the floor
hoping this new twist in plans would work it was time
to leave Virginia but not empty handed, either leave or
spend the rest of her life in a cell working for peanuts
like a Hebrew slave being told when too by CO's, and
how to by CO's and where to by a bitch in a uniform
this was the hell it all boiled down to.

"Baby where going to be rich!" Keisha yelled
out noting even knowing the risk she was involved in.

They both jumped up and down dancing with
each other around the room to an illusion cast by
Solomon.

"Get dress the faster we move the faster we can
get the hell out of town." Danice said.

"Speed kills; remember those old heads use to
tell us that in the hole." Keisha said trying to rekindle
old feelings.

"They were talking about all the speed they smoked, not the speed where about to do." They both laughed.

"I told Solomon I wasn't on paper suppose we get caught?" Keisha said as she stopped dancing and sat down looking worried.

"I told you they were not coming here looking for you so get setup those checks should be rolling in by morning." Danice announced.

The day went smoothly Danice pulled up all the information she would need on the computer while setting up corporate accounts on the other computer. that sat in a Side by Side affect in her office, after she did her job she told Keisha what to wear to the post office and they went to pick up their fake Corporate I.D from one of the ring members who specialized in making them now that everything was set up the checks would be flowing in like milk in the land of milk and honey, Victor who was educated and a inside corporate man who had the degrees and bachelors from some of the finest colleges in America to prove it, he planned on going straight to the top of the Corporate ladder with or without the Corporate worlds help, deals where being made right in front of his nose and he watched as the checks where signed, this deal would be the one to set him and his clique on high from years to come, Solomon was called and waited patiently for the checks to show up once they did they were cashed and the money split.

Keisha became financial unhandi capped over night. She was so caught up in Danice game she ignored taking care of her own business. she left her P.O. hanging mean while the warrants were sent out and pictures of Keisha in her pin stripped suit from Goochland Prison with compliments of Virginia's finest every cop car in the State had her picture posted on their dash boards and informants where on the look out hoping they would see her first for a fix that day. After Solomon paid his accomplices in crime him and Victor left the country to where their bank was stashed in a Swiss bank account, Danice packed all the things she possessed that had sentimental value to her, Keisha grabbed all her new gear shoving them in bags they wanted to leave headed to California to live it up.

Destiny had other plans for their futures.

"I need you to do one more favor before we leave this fucked up town, take my keys to the Jag and ride out to get us some fried chicken, drinks, and what else you think we'll be needing for our trip and here mail this for me." Danice said.

"What's in the envelope, Danice?" Keisha asks.

"Some money for my moms no matter how mad she is at me because of my sexual preference I still send her money. Every time I call her she hangs up on me but I still keep the faith hoping that one day she might change her way of thinking and come back around accepting me as her baby girl.

"She still won't talk to you because you're gay?" Keisha asks.

"No, she so religious she won't see my way as the right way but she's my mother and she need the cash so when ever I pull a job I send her some." Danice answered.

Keisha did as told she speed through the street blasting music. She never felt so free in her life. She pulled up to the Post office and parked the car. She stepped inside the door feeling sexy and cute, she wasn't aware that a list of Virginia's most wanted criminal hung up on the bill boards for all eyes to see. Being a first time felon the thought never crossed her mind after she handed the letter to a white postal inspector he looked over at the bill board and yelled for her to come to back.

"Excuse me ma'am!" He yelled.

The police had been called and her license number wrote down, Keisha drove as fast as she could through the streets trying to get back to Danice place

84

before the cops caught up with her. before she could reach the long drawn out road that lead to the steep hill cop cars 8 deeps sirens blurb out on a high speed chase behind her, she knew it was over at this point but she wasn't willing to stop for none of them do or die was the new way.

"That dumb bitch!" Danice yelled once she heard all the sirens she refused to go down with her. Keisha parked the car bashing it into the garage door. She ran up to the front door crying tears yelling for Danice to let her in, Danice stood in the window pepping out of the side of the blinds. She knew the police would take her to once they came inside the house and seen all the computers with all the information she had obtained for years. Until she let Keisha back in her life Danice ran to the garage and got a rope proceeded to hang herself. She cried before doing so while her girl friend Keisha banged and banged on the door unaware of the damage she had done by not reporting to her P.O. she turned around putting her hands up in the air the police all eight at the same time fired their weapons until they emptied their clips in Keisha's back. She died before her corpus hit the ground.

Chapter 5

Mr. Right

How was she to know he was a con-man?

His words were so beautifully wrote when they appeared on her laptop computer screen. She laid spread eagle on her four poster bed and read the message addressed "Mr. Right" what girl and her right mind wouldn't answer this. Lisa thought to herself as she answered the call. She started her message off hoping one of Miami's desperate housewives didn't beat her to the punch. she needed this at this point and time in her life after the horrific car crash that claimed the life of her husband Marcus, chastity had become away of life to her and a release was in order it was like life was calling her out.

Dear Mister Right: "My name is Lisa and I was wondering are you the one?"...Lisa asks as she smiled and pushed her fingers a little harder writing what was stuck in her brain. She was loaded down with questions hoping to penetrate Mister Right vibes to answer her beck and call her on a positive note. Lisa pushed the send button after she wrote for a full twenty minutes. Asking questions by e-mail with no idea where this man who called himself "Mister Right" came from. She only wished that when he wrote her back his answers to her questions would make her want to pack her shit and go where ever Mister Right was. Being by plane, train, or automobile. Lisa stepped down off her four poster bed and laid out her clothes for the office job at the agency she worked for the last twenty year of her life. This routine was getting boring life called her out along time ago but she refused to buck and live it on the wild side like so many others in her college days.

As she probed the closets for an outfit to wear the next day before her vacation started that's when *"You got mail"* blurted out of the speakers of the laptop that sat on the bed, Lisa ran and glided across the hard wood floors to see was this the message she waited patiently for from Mister Right.

Dear Lisa: "I could only hope I'm the one for you. I'm interested! Lisa is it possible we could meet?"...Mister Right asks Lisa as she sat down on the edge of the bed to read the message as the light from her laptop filled her eyes with a light of hope and a spark of romance, her heart fluttered as she read on.

I can't wait to meet you if you decide to come. I'm grounded looking for a bright beautiful woman to fill my waking hours, are you the one for me? Lisa...Mister Right ended his wishes right there. She thought to herself for a moment "come" this drew a smile to her face, this was exactly what she needed a vacation and a mysterious man full of adventure after all isn't that what life is suppose to be about living. Lisa thought as she started another e-mail hoping Mister Right wasn't some love sick pervert.

Mister Right: Who are you? I think you forgot to post a picture on the message you posted on my web sight and I was also wondering where do you live? More information will be needed since you claim to be the right one for me, are you really? That is the question.

Lisa pushed the send button and waited as she pushed her hips back on the big fluffy pillows that supported her back waiting for an answer she hoped the answer that was to come was one she wanted to hear and not a prankster playing mind games and using the internet to play on innocent woman feelings using them as victims.

Dear Lisa, Here's the picture you asked for.

...The picture that popped up on her screen made Lisa wants to pack her belongings and leave on the first flight out. Mister Right was interesting to the eyes his picture sparked a certain warmth in Lisa's being that made her want to comply with his demands. He was tall dark with a beautiful smile his mustache really set it all off for her. She loved a man with a mustache because of what they are famous for doing with their mouths and every lady knows what that is supposed to be.

Lisa, I can set you up in a luxury hotel with all the fringe benefits just so I can meet you I'm not into looks. I just like your persona and the profile you e-mailed me that why I'm interested in you. I also will pay for your flight out here if that's what you want, is that what you want? I'm a nice guy, Lisa and you'll soon learn this once we meet. I'm looking for a lady to spend a lot of quality time with and from what you're telling me that's what you're looking for also, am I right? I live in New York City and I want you here by my side after all every man needs a good woman are you that woman, Lisa?

Mister Right ended his letter. Lisa sat there in a dream state wondering should she be scare to write back.

Dear Mister Right, I do have some vacation time on my hands as a matter of fact it started today and from the picture you sent me I think we could make a flight reservation at your earliest convenience because I'm coming to New York City. I only pray this is the right decision.

Lisa paused as she took a deep breath.

> **I also need to talk to you by phone so we can confirm everything call me at 305-555-4944 Lisa. I can't wait to hear your voice.**

Lisa sent the message that made her want to meet him even more afterwards she put her luggage on the bed wanting to meet Mister Right he was exactly the type of man she craved in her life. He was interesting and generous offering her vacation package deals in a luxury hotel suite with a round trip ticket from Miami to New York how could and why would she past all this up after all a girl have to live a little in life is what ran rapid through her mind. Lisa could afford to pay for her own vacation if pushed came to shove after all she worked as a Advertising Executive for years she was investment club material, 401K plans was at the top of her portfolio, stocks and bonds, tea bills you name it she had it under her belt and in her safety deposit box at the local bank. Money wasn't an issue. Single with no children was at the top of profile page but life wasn't what she had summed it all up to be she planned her future in her youthful years during her college days life was what you make it if your willing to take a chance at least that's what she was told her husband Marcus death really made her throw herself into her work head first over the years. She saved all the money she could like the world was coming to an abrupt end. Lisa slept knowing she would call out sick the following the morning and start her vacation time early a shopping spree was in order. She spent the whole day maxing out credit cards to make the right first impression on the man that called himself Mister Right. His picture made her want to do this and the fact that he worked in the financial district of Wall Street in Manhattan. Turned her on this was the man of her dreams. She was so excited about her new adventure she forgot to ask Mister Right his real name. She knew he would eventually call back if he really wanted to meet her like he claimed. Lisa stepped back and grasped her heart as the tiffany lamp that sat on the table spun all its colors were illuminating things where moving extremely fast the way she acted over this man Mister Right. She hadn't even met or spoke with him over the phone yet. Could she have been that desperate like so many other desperate housewives in Miami that she would sacrifice her life to be loved by an internet predator? She would create in her mind that Mister Right was the right man before hand; the next morning she wondered into Victoria Secret wanting to buy lingerie to set the wheels in motion once she reached the big apple. If thing went right she would seduce and mold her man into the man she wanted him to be. That being a man with a hard on for her and her only she would make Mister Right "The One". The stores where crowded along the Miami Beach front as Lisa shopped maxing out a couple of credit cards. That already was on there last leg. She bought a couple of the latest designer teddy's along with satin kimono's and bra and panty set's that would set the mood if she chose too. She shopped at the top designer stores from Gucci to Ralph Laurens and Burberry's to get some of the latest trends she had seen in catalog. She wanted outfits that would reveal lots of brown skin which she planned on showing; this vacation would be one to remember if she had her way. Lisa arrived back at her Ocean front Apartment in a condo on Collins Avenue one of Miami's most wanted areas to live in. Her tri-level penthouse apartment with the ocean view was considered one of the hottest finds for a forty year old all alone in the world.

Lisa opened the door walking into pitch black darkness after she returned from her shopping spree. As she stepped into her apartment the smell of fresh roses that sat in a vase near the front door hit her nose. She closed the double doors behind her and kicked off her brand new pair of Manolo's Blahnik heels that she paid $495 for maxing out her American Express to purchase. Just as she did the phone rang.

"Hello" Lisa said as she walked throughout her condo turning on lights and stripping to change her clothes.

"Lisa?" The Deep sensual voice said in a soft tone hypnotizing his subject without even trying. As she switched him over to the intercom system.

"Who's calling?" Lisa asks with uncertainty in her voice.

"This is Clint." The voice said with a sexy deepness to it. Clint's voice could penetrate the weakest woman and make her weak in the knees while at the same time gaining her confidence. He used his gift of gab well while seducing his vulnerable victim.

"What? Lisa asks as she stood up to attention unconsciously bending to Clint's demands with sensual undertones without even knowing.

"I wanted you to know everything's set your flight leaves tomorrow at noon. I hoped you wouldn't mind the timing being so soon considering your vacation time is here as you stated in your e-mail. I must say Lisa you're a piece of work and I can't wait to see you." Lisa heart dropped Mister Right aka Clint melted the receiver right in the palm of Lisa's hands. She kicked her Prada bags to the side pushing them against the bed as she sat down in her Ralph Lauren wing back chair spreading her legs while throwing one over the arm of the chair. Listening at full attention to the voice whose arms she couldn't wait to lay in at least that was the picture in her fantasy.

"What time does the flight leave?" Lisa asks while envisioning herself sitting on a first class flight to the big apple fantasy was something she indulged in well.

"Noon, I will be expecting you to step off that plane and meet me near the luggage check." Clint said with authority in his voice and she loved the force he used when dealing with her.

"Well...I guess it's settled then. I'll see you tomorrow Clint and please tell me this is not a mistake. I'm taking a big chance with you and I hope it pans out right, who know you just might be the man I been looking for." Lisa said feeling Mister Right out the conversation would have to last for more than five minutes for her to make a final decision and the right questions would have to be asked she waited anticipating Clint's answer.

"I have reservations set up for you at the Palace Hotel located in the Ritziest part of Madison Avenue and dinner at the Glitz." Clint said as all became silent and Lisa the same. She could feel Clint's vibes in her ear drums as he talked her pussy jumped knowing how bad she needed his touch he turned her on by the motions he penetrated thus far and it was obvious." I'll be there." Lisa said making her closing statement before the dial tone over powered her. Lisa made all the right preparations for her trip she backed tracked to assure her ticket would be at the airport as she was told by Clint she wrote her flight number down morning couldn't come fast enough. As the sun finally popped out of the sky she woke up sitting on the side of her bed sleeping in the nude was not a strange thing to Lisa. She walked through her apartment wearing a pair of gold thong before sitting her Louis Vuitton luggage by the front door. before doing her morning ritual that consist of a layout of yoga stretches Lisa did what came naturally first the tree pose while gazing out at the ocean as the waves crashed during high tide on this sunny Miami morning. Pictures of the big apple played a major role in the stream of pictures that played out in her mind and its reputation for being bad. she could only hope Mister Right aka Clint's status as a financial advisor in the financial district of Wall Street was the only thing that brought on feelings of security after working around white collar men all of her life she could only image his behavior and his attitude. His laptop would probably be part of the date with him checking the Dow every chance he get (Lisa laughed) just thinking about it. She made sure everything she would need was packed before leaving her apartment headed for the Miami International Airport. She walked through the airport rushing. She stepped in line with the rest of the passengers to board the plane after checking her ticket for it' seating number she seen the number thirty and figured it had to be mistake after all she knew she was first class ticket material. Clint was yet to learn this she walked slowly down the isle only to end up in the back of the plane staring at the wing blocking her view. Lisa couldn't believe she wasn't sitting in first class seat sipping champagne this blew her mind the plane took off as she sat there steaming inside wondering in the deep ruins of her mind was this forgivable then she came to the conclusion" yes" it was and nothing was going to make her turn back now not after coming thus far the plane finally pulled into LaGuardia International Airport with a bumpy landing. she held on to her seat with fear in her heart hoping Clint would be there waiting patiently like he told her he would be when she arrived at the luggage claim. She searched her purse for Clint's photo only to find that it was left at home. she stood there shifting her head from one side to the other waiting and watching trying to remember his face she looked on as passengers who boarded her flight met up with love ones, Clint watched on like a voyeur waiting to see if she would notice him, he giggled as she stood there looking like a lost child who had been abandoned by her parents...

"Excuse me." Clint said as he walked up smiling.

"Hi." Lisa said amazed at how handsome he was in person.

"You look like a lost child standing there." Clint said as he reached for her luggage.

"I felt lost for a minute. I finally get to meet you Mister Right aka Clint." Lisa said as she reached to help with the luggage.

"I hoped you would come." Clint said as he gazed into Lisa's eyes making the feelings of melting arise deep inside of her.

As Clint and Lisa walked through the electronic sliding door there was a horse and carriage sitting there in front of the airport in the mitts of traffic. Lisa stepped out into the street walking pass it.

"Oh...I forgot to mention this is for you!" Clint opened the door to the carriage as Lisa sat down on the velour red velvet seats not seeing the roses she sat on.

"Wow...is these for me? You sure know how to make a first impression. Do you do this for all your dates that come in from out of town?" Lisa said waiting for a response.

"You would be the first, Lisa." Clint said as he took hold of her hand as she gripped the bunch of roses. Lisa didn't know whether she should comply with his move or just let it flow; as he touched her she could feel herself getting hot and bothered as her body talked to her. Her wild side that she tried for years to keep dormant sneaking up on her the feeling was so strong it scared her.

"I have a room at the Palace nothing but the best for you, Lisa once you get inside to freshen up we have reservations set up for two at the Glitz as I mentioned on the phone, Oh yeah Lisa welcome to the big apple the city that never sleeps." Clint said as he planted a wet kiss on Lisa's cheek trying to make her feel comfortable as if he had known her for years.

"I've been fighting with myself on whether I should forgive you for that horrible seat on the plane but I guess this makes up for it." Lisa said as she looked into Clint's big brown eyes.

Just as the horse and carriage galloped down the street behind cars cluttering the streets you could hear the music from its huffs clinging to the cements roads. The traffic was thick just as the red light changed, a black Lexus Pulled up with tinted windows Clint looked over into the window on the drivers side it came halfway down the driver of the car was a beautiful hard body blonde wearing black leather attire she looked at Lisa as if she was under inspection before the car pulled off leaving smoke from its exhaust in the face of the horse carriage driver and its passengers.

"What was that all about?" Lisa said before she turned back in Clint's direction to resume the conversation about how he was going to spoil her while she was there in New York. She would be wined and dined by the man who called himself Mister Right and this is just what she need. Could he read her mind he knew he had to gain Lisa confidence and from where Clint sat that would be easy considering she was a lonely desperate housewife over forty or just pushing it she would be a prime target for the game that was about to be played her portfolio and profile was just what Clint and his crew was looking for forty, successful, single, no children, Advertising Executive money was written all over Lisa's chest in invisible letters in dollar signs Clint knew he had him a winner now all he needed to do was get her to drop her defenses and she would be his for the taking.

"So...Clint you're more than I expected. I think we are going to get along just fine even though I never would have considered coming this far for a man the only thing that sold me was the fact that you have a beautiful profile and your job description is awesome.

"Well, thank you Lisa, yours is just as awesome but that's enough about me I can't wait to show you what us New Yorkers are all about and I also can't wait to show you what the night holds for you and I." Clint said looking sexy in Lisa's eyes as he grabbed hold of her hand.

Lisa smiled she didn't know how to respond just as the horse and carriage pulled up to the curb of one of the Cities most famous Hotels the Palace two bell hops ran over to the passengers to take control of their luggage and roll them into the Palace on dollies.

"This is it...do you like it?" Clint asks holding Lisa's hand.

"Of course... I can tell it's the best." Lisa said as she looked up and seen how tall the sky scraper hotel stood all forty eight floors.

Clint took her by the hand and guided her inside to the counter of the famous hotel he registered her in and received her key card.

"I hate to rush you but our dinner reservations are in ten minutes." Clint announced.

Lisa stood there and watched as her luggage left her sight being carted up stairs Clint moved so fast she tried to keep up.

"Now we won't be late for dinner?" Clint said as he moved like a Wall Street stock broker on the floor of the exchange making deals with other people's money.

Clint led the way he opened the doors to the Glitz the atmosphere was unbelievable the music soft and the cliental sophisticated the lights were soft as the food and laughter filled the air. The waitresses pranced around in their black and white sexy uniforms with ruffled behinds seducing the customers.

"You really know how to spread the charm.' Lisa said as Clint pulled her chair out like a gentleman.

"The night is still young and I have so much to show you. Once the night is over you'll know the real me." Clint said looking shifty eyed, the waitress took their orders and brought over a bottle of the hotels best bubbly and a bottle of patron for Clint's approval it was as if he was a special client in the house with the treatment he received, Lisa just sat back and enjoyed herself feeling just as special.

"I never once thought I would end up in Manhattan on my vacation if it hadn't been for you Clint I'd still be shacked up in my quaint condo in Miami or who knows where I'd be. Your e-mail really grabbed my attention why would a man as sexy as you be looking for a date over the internet? After all you're a financial broker you should be married or something." Lisa said while scanning the menu to order. Clint smiled for he knew the truth and Lisa was yet to learn his philosophy Lisa was at the top of his project list she would be taken on a ride concerning the matters of the heart and the pocket book by the time she left New York City her whole world would be turned upside down.

"I like you Lisa you are just the type of woman I want to spend time with at least a couple of days, do you think you can stay for a couple of days or will you be rushing back to Miami? (Clint took hold of her hand once again) look at you your beautiful, Lisa." Clint said as he picked her hand up off the table and strokes it gently like a gentleman. Lisa melted at his touch. she blushed as Clint stroked her ego as well, she wanted to re-acted what she was feeling deep inside at that moment by physically jumping over the table and tackling him to the floor and ripped his clothes off but that would have to wait if Clint played his cards right that would naturally happen by the end of the night, love had nothing to do with it. "May I be excuse I have to use the little girl's room?" Lisa said before standing up and making her way gracefully across the room. She had no way of knowing that the room she walked across so gracefully was inhabited by con-man and con- woman like the house of game. When Lisa stepped foot out the restroom the whole atmosphere in the Glitz had changed the lights where a whole complete different color and the music had sped up from piano jazz to a hipper tone the group that gathered at the Glitz at this point was a more swinging crowd and the look was more that of a club atmosphere then that of a restaurant. the bar was packed with woman sitting there waiting to be approached by available men with money and tantalized for the night Lisa looked around and noticed the metamorphosis that had taken place since she stepped foot in the restroom. as she walked towards the table she left Clint seated as. a size two brunette with big boobs had beat her to the punch back to the table the brunette was leaning over kissing Mister Right on the lips and he complied while looking Lisa dead in her eyes. As she approached the table all that was gathered there disbursed.

"Don't mind her she's just an old friend I haven't seen in years." Clint said as he stood up ready to leave the Glitz.

The night pass by so fast time seemed too sped up since she stepped foot off the plane she hadn't time to freshen up or even see the inside of her hotel room she pulled the card Clint gave her to open her door out of her purse when he finally decided to let her go upstairs.

"I'm going to let you go up to your room and freshen up and I'll meet you here in thirty minutes I have a couple of loose ends to tighten up before I take you to one of my favorite clubs. The night is still young and god knows there is so much to see, see you in thirty. Clint said before walking towards the Glitz swinging door Lisa looked at him from the corner of her eyes wondering would he meet up with the brunette as she stepped onto the elevator with the elevator man as the doors closed Clint looked back and smiled.

Lisa room number was in big red numbers on the card. She stepped off and practically ran to her room to shower since Clint insists she meet him in the lobby in thirty minutes. She Opened the door running straight for her luggage in the corner and throw them both on the bed, Mister Right was hot his eyes were beautiful not to mention his conversation smooth just the type of man she'd have to watch. Other woman already tried to approach him in the restaurant this was not happening tonight while at the club she found the most outrageously sexy outfit she spent hundreds of dollars on that would knock Clint's socks off her back would have to be completely out and her shoes sexy showing her ankles and legs this is where Minolo Blanik heels came in her maxed out American Express card would not had been spent in vain. Her perfume would have to be just right after all aroma therapy played a major role in her life and she wanted to share her hopes and dreams with her new man. Just as she stepped into her pantyhose the phone rang.

"It's me, Lisa." Clint said in a rushing voice as if he was being chased by an angry mob.

"I'll be down in a minute, Clint I hope I'm wearing the right thing considering I don't know what kind of club where going too." Lisa said.

"I'm sure what ever your wearing is sexy." Clint replied as he stood there on his cell phone by the cab waiting for her to get off the elevator patiently.

The elevator doors opened and Lisa stepped off wearing her midnight blue dress with the back out and her Minolo Blanik shoes this really set it all off. Clint's mouth hung open as he watched her walk across the floor like a Manhattan model he liked what he seen and it showed on his face. She was worth a million bucks in his eyes from her taste in clothing he stood there and held the door open as Lisa shuck her ass walking to the cab

"Is this dress sexy enough, Clint?' Lisa asks as she plopped down on the leather seats in the New York City cab.

"The club I'm taking you to is one of he hottest clubs in Manhattan and I hope it's sophisticated enough for you." Clint said as he sat down beside Lisa.

The cab pulled off with tremendous force leaving Lisa and Clint holding on to the door handles as it turned the corner.

"Hey... slow down driver what's the rush!" Clint yelled through the partition as the cabby took instruction well and slowed down while Clint gave him the destination in which he wanted to go.

"19 West 24th Street." Clint ordered and the cabby listened.

The cabby doubled back and swerved around the corner like a bat out of hell headed to the cutting room the club Clint wanted to go.

"Are you both a couple of Celebes?" The cab driver asks.

"No we're not." Clint said.

"That sounds like an interesting club are you a regular." Lisa asks as she looked around at the scenery as the cab speeded down Broadway.

"I try to be a regular you know how it is when you have to be on the floor of the stock exchange revved up and ready to go first thing in the morning that's enough about me what kind of lifestyle are you into?" Clint asks waiting to hear the boring answer.

"I usually spend a lot of time at the office especially since the death of Marcus, I basically been saving my money and working hard, that's all until you." Lisa said smiling from ear to ear as she slowly but surely begun to trust Clint more and more she disclosed her financial information with out thinking of the consequences of her actions.

"I know how it is to loose someone close to you. I had a lost my self but I rather not talk about it right now. the club I'm taking you too is one of the best kept little secrets in Manhattan, the stars hang out here." The cab came to a complete stop in the front of a quaint café style bar front when Lisa stepped out of the cab Clint touched her behind and smiled she

100

turned in his direction and smiled back. She walked arm and arm with Clint to the front of the club as the door swung open they both stepped into the club where the music was live and the celebrities were definitely in the house. Lisa couldn't believe her eyes as she gazed over to the bar she seen a one of her favorite Celebes sitting there in deep conversation with one of the clubs regulars like it was nothing, Lisa shuck Clint's arm trying to get his attention to show him her discovery only to find him whispering sweet nothings in a blondes ear.

"The music is blasting talk to me later." Clint said as he walked onto the dance floor with the blonde head woman leaving Lisa seated at the big mahogany bar alone three seats from the movie star.

"Will you be drinking alone this evening?" The bartender asks.

"I'll have a cocktail, thank you." Lisa said feeling voided out and abandoned.

She watched on as the slow song that played brought Clint and the blonde headed woman closer together on the dance floor their bodies clung close as the song played on the heat between them was enough to set the dance floor on fire.

"That was supposed to be my dance." Lisa whispered to herself as she gulped down her cocktail with lightening speed and ask the bartender for another one to chase away her blues.

"How about something stronger, ma'am?" the bartender asks as he brought over a bottle of scotch sitting it in front of Lisa as if she was an alcoholic.

After the song Clint made his way back to the bar alone the blonde had left the cutting room to go elsewhere.

"Would you like to dance?" Clint asks as he walked up on Lisa.

"You have a nerve to ask me now!" Lisa yelled feeling tipsy from the two cocktails and the scotch she was pissed with Clint for disrespecting her.

101

"I know woman. What do you want me to say this is who I am, and there is no way I'm willing to change for you or no other woman." Clint said with a loud voice over the music and the arguing attracting attention Lisa favorite stars attention she looked over at them shaking her head along with half the cutting rooms guest.

Lisa stood up. she couldn't believe the bass Clint was using in his voice, Lisa ran outside feeling humiliated and embarrassed she flagged down a cab as tears ran down her cheeks Clint wasn't far behind he would have to apologize if he was to get what he wanted from Lisa this is where plan B came in.

Lisa arrived back at the Palace Hotel mad as hell. She stormed upstairs by way of elevator and opened her room door. She slammed it behind her not caring who heard it she ran over to her bed and laid on it trying to come to her senses Clint had hit a nerve. Clint came to the door with a bottle of fine wine and another bunch of roses trying to make up where he went wrong.

"Lisa!" He yelled as he knocked on the door hoping Lisa would open it.

"I don't have anything left to say to you it's obvious you're not the one for me Mister Wrong!" Lisa yelled back standing on the opposite side of the door hurt and humiliated.

"Please let me make up for the way I behaved tonight." Clint said with his head pressed against the door while holding his hands with the bottle of wine and roses behind his back. He had to get inside in order to get what the job he was on required and that was check books, credit cards, debit cards, and what ever other financial monetary unit and information Lisa Possessed Being a con-man was a hard game and Clint played it well he would get what he wanted if it meant murder.

Lisa wiped her eyes letting him in.

"I'm sorry for the way I treated you at the club and I will do what ever it takes to make it up to you, Lisa." Lisa loved the way he said her name with his hard core New York City accent it turned her on she looked into his eyes.

"I'm also sorry I made you cry that is the last thing I wanted to do." Clint said lying through his teeth. He knew in order to get the job done he would have to be where the money was that being her hotel room. This is where plan B came in humiliation was a part of the game. "Leave the club and take her back to the hotel room" is what the blonde told Clint after all she was the leader of the whole ring and when she gave an order it had to be followed if Clint was to remain a part of her crew.

Lisa stood there waiting for him to make his peace just when she thought he did, he grabbed her and passionately kissed her on the lips creating the mood for love making this was also a part of the game getting the victim emotionally attached then take them over completely.

"I," Lisa said not able to get the complete sentence out of her mouth. Clint scooped her up off the floor and carried her over to the bed laying her on it; Lisa volunteering unzipped her dress letting it fall to the floor. Clint stood there fully erect hoping he would be able to drive her crazy in bed. He begin to strip he took his silk shirt off laying it on the chair like the GQ man he was supposed to be. he laid his slacks over the arm of the chair straightening out any wrinkles that may have formed while on his body, Lisa laid their in her Victoria Secret silk undies with her breast exposed waiting for him to touch her all over her body this is what she wanted soon as she seen him in the airport but the time wasn't right.

"I like you, Lisa and even if I'm not the right one for you, I want you." Clint took both his hand squeezing her breast close together before taking his mouth and opening it wide begin to suck them licking each one individually with precise detail.

"I knew you where good when I laid eyes on you." Clint said in a whisper.

Lisa couldn't take the anticipation any longer she got up off the bed and stood up for Clint to enter her from the back. She knew this position would leave him open wanting more this was a proven theory she learned from being married to Marcus for so long, If Mister Right wasn't for her at least she would leave a lasting impression on his brain. They made love for hours leaving them both sweaty and wet.

"I'm going to take a shower, Clint would you like to join me?" Lisa asks as she put on her silk red kimono and slippers to match.

"I'll join you in a minute." Clint said as he rolled off the bed as soon as the bathroom door closed he made his way across the room straight to Lisa's pocketbook he opened it and found her wallet emptying it's contents all over the floor. He took her master card, visa, discover card, American express that had been maxed out unbeknown to Clint, he shoved all the spoils in his pockets, he knew a woman of Lisa financial status had to have more than this and he was going to find it. Clint listened in to see if the water had stopped running before making his way across the floor to hit up her luggage, Lisa had no idea her Mister Right turned out to be Mister Wrong with an insatiable appetite for ripping off woman he lured to New York City leaving them high and dry.

"Clint, are you coming in the shower with me, Honey?" Lisa yelled through the bathroom door.

"I'll be right there, baby." Clint said as he cracked the door telling her he was on the telephone.

Lisa stood there with hot water running down her face thinking she was in love and maybe her calling Clint Mister Wrong was wrong after all he made her feel good in bed like no other. No one had made her feel this way in years, naïve to the game of con she stood there thinking Clint cared for her because she gave him good sex. When this was not the problem Clint search Lisa things until he come to the conclusion he took everything that was worth something once this was established he put his clothes on and left leaving a note of surprise behind.

Lisa called out for him one more time before getting out of the shower dripping wet walking to the bathroom door to open it, once she did she noticed her luggage thrown in the corner open with her clothes laying all over the place and all her jewelry was gone. she ran to her pocket book to find all her credit cards gone and all of her cash, along with her ticket Clint had brought her to come to New York City as she stood there letting the towel fall to the floor butter ball naked she walked over to the hotel phone that sat on the table and discovered a note laying on the bed wrote in big red letters the note read.

Dear Lisa,

I'm sorry I'm not the right one for you but there is something I want to say to you and I hope it don't break your heart or change your life for the worst but I forgot to tell you I have HIV the virus that cause AIDS.

Clint aka Mister Right.

Chapter 6

For Love or Money

The night was hectic while the DEA agents stood at the front door holding the last ounce of Ya Yo in their hands. Melody was humble she been through this one before. It was just a matter of time; she stood there thinking if only she'd listened by hiding the Ya-Yo like her man Toni told her to this nightmare wouldn't have happened. Following five children through the house on a twenty four hour a day basis made it impossible to think. The snitches they paid dope to on the regular was suppose to warn them but didn't. Like the pit bulls did in the front yard. The head of the posse of DEA agents claimed she found an extra ounce in the back yard in the dog house during her search. "How could that be"? Melody said in a loud angry voice. The cop cuffed her boyfriend first he was sort after as public enemy number #1. This was a trophy to the cops payday had come. The Social Service worker took each one of the children stuffing them in a vehicle as Melody watched on in silence. She was powerless to the forces of the government; Melody looked on silently as her man and head drug dealer on the block dealing hashish, Meth, crack and a variety of other drugs for the last ten year. He yelled for her to make sure she posts all his money on his canteen fund by morning. Melody felt as if she was dead smack in the middle of a gangsta movie she ignored the cry of the kids and the cry's of her man. The police pushed her on the top of her head pushing her down into the police car as he slammed the door in her face. She would be to be taken down town to the nearest police station. Where she would be shoved in a dirty cell while waiting to be processed and transported to where ever she had a warrant. Melody looked on as the Social Service vehicle cruised out of sight with all five of her babies in the back seat. She knew they would be probe by these government officials looking to end another black family's reign. She turned around restrained by her cuffs unable to see the outcome of her man Toni's arrest. She just heard his moans to be set free. Knowing once the police cruiser pulled off and turned the corner she wouldn't see Toni for a long time. It was already discussed night after night for a long time between Toni and her during fist fights meanly while he had her in a compromising positions either with his foot in her back or his fist in her mouth.

"Which precinct are you taking me too?" Melody asked in a low solemn voice.

The officer gave her a dirty look (he hated niggas) she remembers him from the last bust that took place just last week. This made her sit back and shut her mouth completely. She let the chip fall where they may. She and Toni had been riding dirty for so long she felt this bust before it came but never took the proper provisions to make sure it never hit home. Her oldest daughter Monica was schooled on how to answer question from the Social Service agency once they probed her to tell her mother's business. She taught her to never snitch on family for fear of never seeing them again. She schooled her on what the workers goals were. which was to break up families after Melody told the story this became a part of her five daughter's make up. Her mother made sure she made that point each and everyday to each one of her children like a ritual. The one thing that brought her a streak of joy was the fact that ten thousand dollars was supposed to be stashed away

And she planned on using it to start over. Returning to the house was priority number one.

Once she made bail. The night was long and cold; and she was locked up in the worst jail in the Washington DC on Pennsylvania Ave. which made her want to go home even faster. The judge pats her on the wrist during her pre trail hearing releasing her to light probationary sentence luck was on her side in the eye of adversity. How easy Melody thought to herself as she stepped outside the dirty court house with praises in her heart and an empty pocket-book and the fact that she didn't have her children ate at her heart. She planned on visiting her man Toni in the county jail to show her love and support all the while representing for the family during this temporary set back in their lives. Sticking together was king at times like these this is the way she was taught to stand by her man after growing up in the hood all her life. Toni waited to be sentenced and transported out of state to a prison for his repeat felonies with drug dealing charges this would probably be the physical death of him. This was the last thing Melody needed right now in her life Toni with a forty year sentence this couldn't happen she would rather be dead right now then face that moment in time and history but she knew it was coming sooner rather than later. Toni paced the floor in his cell trying to figure out when his contract with Satan ran out because his demons had finally caught up with him. His distrust to himself and his woman made him vowed to himself to tell Melody the truth once and for all about the relationship him and her best friend were involved in and the birth of a baby was the result. Melody walked into the county jail feeling extremely empty and low with hopes of being told Toni had a stash of money for her and the children to lay back on while he did his time like he usually did each and every time he got popped. The judge was certain to throw the book at him for a long time on this run. Toni walked up to the partition that stood between him and Melody as the officer took his cuffs off. He took his seat on the cold steel bench. His orange jumper he sported like a designer pair of Jeans with the jail logo on the back represented his place of residency and his future place of dwelling for his unorganized drug dealing practices. The judge gave him an appointment for a date to be sentenced. Melody took her seat feeling fortunate to be sitting on the opposite side of the partition and not in the same predicament as Toni.

"Toni, when is the hearing, baby. I promise you I'll be there. Is there any body you need me to call for you, honey?" Melody asks trying to be a pillow of support for her man and the father of her children.

"I have something to tell you. I know you're not going to like it. But this is just the way it is right now at least until I get out of here. I want Karen in the house by the time I get out (Toni said holding his head down before looking in Melody's eyes to see her re-action) and if I don't get out. I want her and my son to live in my house I paid for with my blood, sweat, and tears money!" Toni knew he had just snatched Melodies heart right out the center of her chest like the heretic. He looked at the mother of his five daughters like a piece of dirt with a smirk on his face. As she sat there unable to speak from the electrical bolt of lighting that ran through her heart from the death blow and sentence Toni had just sentenced her to.

"If you would have hid the yayo, I wouldn't be here in jail right now; you need to learn how to listen. Melody and since you didn't listen to what I told you then maybe just maybe you'll listen to what I'm about to say. I been doing your best friend Karen for ten years now and the baby she's carrying around on her hip on the regular, that's my baby. (Toni puffed his chest out to show his proud father ego while talking about his first born son) I want you out of my house!" Toni stood up hitting the plastic glass window that stood between him and a slap from Melody. He stood there with a big wide grin on his face and kicked the metal bench before he pimped back through the door walking with the corrections officer that navigated him back to his cell. Melody sat there with tears forming in the corner of her eyes waiting for Toni to make a u-turn. She couldn't comprehend what Toni had just said it hadn't calculated in her head. He wasn't saying anything she hadn't heard on the streets for along time from all his woman that wanted him. It was like a second skin that she always blocked out when other females talked about it. She always played dumb to the facts while still pumping his babies like stair steppers. He had another seed what drug dealer didn't? Melody thought to herself as she thought about all of Toni's friends she had fucked on the sly while his back was turned, his sin was forgivable. Just when the doors closed Melody got the message she jumped up and hit the plastic glass she noticed the jilt to the heart Toni had just hit her with like a black Dracula before he ran like he was so use to doing all of his life.

"Toni!" Melody yelled turning the heads of the other inmate's visitors who had come to the jail house to visit their peoples.

Melody cried as she made her way through the parking lot wondering where to go next. Her man of ten years wanted her out of the house and out in the cold with five girls and no money, she prayed as she cruised down the street hurt from the confession that hit her like a vampire stake to the heart. What she had with Toni was not there anymore he was disloyal to her and she wanted to die at this very moment. She hoped the ten thousand dollars she stashed in the back of the draw in her bedroom would still be there when she returned to the house. If one of Toni junkie brothers didn't beat her to the punch. All the junkies in the neighborhood came sniffing around looking for loose ends turning over furniture looking for something to resell for a quick crack. They wanted everything the cops didn't confiscate while Melody was locked up in the county jail. By the time Melody pulled up to the drive way of her house, Toni's new bitch had a moving van pulled up to the front door directing the mover where to put her furniture. Melody's Lexus stop cold in the front of the big brick house, as she jumped out of the car ready to fight with her best friend who stood there profiling with Melody's man's baby on her hip.

"You Bitch!" You were fucking him all the time, huh!" Melody yelled to the top of her lung with her fist balled up ready to initiate the first blow; all the moving men stepped to the side while both women let off much needed steam in the front yard kicking and screaming while pulling on each others weave calling each other out their name wanting to kill each other like to vicious pit bulls.

"Don't you see it in his eyes and check out his mouth? This is Toni's baby, bitch" Karen screamed as she stood there with her hair all over her head, she grabbed for little Tee and placed him on her hip while pointing at his eyes and mouth trying to prove a point. Melody loss all sense of control and all rules of reason before commencing to kicking her ex- best friends Karen's ass in the front yard.

"You fell to realize he had five daughters by me! I gave up my dreams to be with Toni and to sell dope and maneuver a bunch of junkie all day every day of my life for ten years. And to think I shared all my dreams with my best friend all the while you were jealous of me. This is the thanks I get, huh. If I would have known you were hating on me I would have been kicked your ass. Melody went off at this point the police were called as the mover pulled her off of Karen all the neighbors on the block stood in their front yard acting as if they were watering grass, or picking up trash to see the fight, the things the neighborhood knew had come to pass while becoming a slap of reality to Melody. Everybody on the block knew her man was banging her best friend for years she was the only one wearing blinders. No one would step forth to tell her the one thing she didn't see, she thought she would have a nervous breakdown right there in the arms of the cop that rushed over to hold her up after she fell backwards.

"That bitch is moving in my house!" Melody yelled as the police cuffed her waiting for her to cool down before setting her free.

Melody remained on the scene in the cop car cooling down watching the cop write his report from the window.

"I want a restraining order against her!" Karen yelled as she picked up a brick off the ground showing it to Melody as a means to a threat.

"That's my house, how are you going to let her move in my house! Melody asks the cop as she tried to get out of the cop car ready to fight again for what she believed in but the door wouldn't open.

Karen stood there holding Melody's man baby on her hips gazing into the cop cruisers window mussing the fire already set as she smiled in her face knowing Toni wouldn't be out for a long time after all he was public enemy number one and with a rep like his he couldn't complain. His property had become a real menace in his community being the crack spot for junkies and playing loud gangsta music through out the neighborhood some times all night long. Not to mention the complaints from all the neighbors were rolling in at the local precinct on a regular basis complaint about the music, the junkies, and the action that went on everyday all daylong. Melody silent freaked her out. She planned on taking matter into her own hands. While she sat there quite until the police decided to let her go. She knew in order to get inside of the house to get her stashed money she would have to break in.

"That's all right, bitch. I got you." Melody said before getting in her Lexus driving off in a rage with revenge plus murder on her mind. She cruise the streets not knowing where to go except up and down the streets of Washington DC Northeast side with out any type of plan. She thought about all the money they blew on pure none- sense and the way she took care of other people and now that she needed some one there was no one there for her. She cried as she listened to the slow jam CD that she played on her state of the art sound system Toni installed just yesterday. The drug money she made on the regular while slinging dope with and for Toni for years was wearing thin and she doubted Toni would give her any since his feeling towards her and his five daughter's had grown cold. All the things she knew that she could black-mail him with faded out of her thought waves in fear of taking the fall with Toni. She thought about his new woman with his baby sitting there in her dream house this brought on the feeling of wanting to kill something. She cried and prayed hoping an angel heard her pray little did Melody know The house was not taken over by the DEA because it was not in Toni's name but in the name of his first born son, the paper for a change had been drawn up by Karen his new woman and Melody's best friend. Unbeknown to Melody, Toni and his new woman plotted behind her back for month ending with her eviction. Melody had no family except a eighty year old aunt that was scared to open her door anyone after a certain hour, She pulled her car around the corner from the house and sat there thinking about death and how she wished she was dead because she felt used up, hurt, crushed and a variety of other emotions ran through her veins. She cried and took hold of a gun that she kept in the glove compartment while walking on the side of the house in the alleyway. The house she raise her five children in she only knew the in's and out's of the property, she took hold of the gun walking slowly trying not to be seen by no one and climbed into an open window she left open in case of emergencies.

"Thank you." Karen said before locking the door behind the movers. She was about to put her son to bed and take a shower in her new bathroom. Melody laid low in the closet in the kitchen waiting for the perfect moment to make a move and get her money from behind the draw in the bed room as Karen closed the bathroom door and walked into the walk in shower. Melody ran up the stairs to get her money she flipped the dresser over only to discover the money was not there anymore someone had beat her to the punch. She wanted to murder Karen deep down inside for what she done to her and her children by seducing her man and taking over what she thought was rightfully hers. But how could she explain that to a court of law one she got caught with the murder weapon in her hands after the fact Melody crept through the hallway past the bathroom while listened in as Karen sung while in the shower. Before she walked to the bedroom her small child laid in that use to be her daughter's room. She pushed the door halfway open peeping in before closing it back. The steps crept as she snuck down them on the way out of the front door. Her life had been filled with horrors every since Toni been in her life ands knocked her up with his seed. He seduced her right in front of her mother's house while

Her mother watched on not really caring. His state of the art yellow sports raced down the block of her street, Toni's had a sexy smile with his diamond fronts that gleaming colors of yellow, blue, red, green from the sun ignorant to the chain of events that took place in the world for the diamond's to reach Toni's mouth. He knew how to work his beautiful muscle built body he knew he could make any young girl drool over his anatomy and make them give it up in the blink of an eye. Either he would buy them a pair of air force ones hyping them up for their virginity or they'd end up pregnant and was stuck with him and his spawn for life. Learning how to numb feeling was something a young girl like Melody's found hard to do she was goo-goo eyed over Toni's anatomy her self and (refused to take a bow from his presents like the show was over. this is what ran though her mind as she daydreamt) everything in their relationship had become so predictable up until this point. Reality was hard enough without day dreaming.

Melody had to find a base for her children once she picked them up from the Social Service the following day like the judge order she could do. Pulling up to the Mayflower inn she sat in the car watching the motels guest as they checked in and out of rooms an old man who appeared to be alone stepped out of one of the rooms ready to check out. He turned in his keys to the main office before casing the parking lot for beggars and thugs before sojourning to his Chrysler New Yorker that was parked near by. Melody walked beside the front window on the driver's side of the car and knocked looking shivering from the cold.

The man jumped from being startled.

"Excuse me, sir!" Melody said knocking trying to get the strange man to open his window before driving off.

"I need a place to stay. Sir can you help me! I have no money could you please help me, sir I'll do anything you need me-too." Melody yelled loud enough for his ears only as she stood there crying to the top of her lungs, her teddy bear face always drew attention, The middle aged man held his head down from feeling sorry for the black lost woman that wanted his attention.

"What do you want me to do are you on crack or something?" The small frame black man asked as he starts his Chrysler New York and pulled the lever ready to drive away.

"No, my children's father just put me out of my house for my best friend he broke the news to me

115

tonight before he put me out and she had his baby!" Melody yelled before breaking down in the parking lot.

"What do you want from me lady?" The strange said before he tried to roll his window up.

"All I'm asking for is your help. If you are a Christian man like that bible that laid on the seat suggests then you'll help me at least get a room." Melody said laying a guilt trip on the Christian man as he stepped out the car ready to assist. The middle aged man looked at Melody from head to toe before he walked into the motel office and paid for the same room he had just left.

"What ever you are doing out here in the streets you need to give it up, because the streets are designed to mess up lives." The man said before revealing that he was a preacher Melody shook his hand before closing the door of her room.

Toni laid in his cell knowing that once the judge seen his face walk into his court room he would do the fifty- five year that he promised him at his last conviction hearing. Karen was the kind of woman he always had in the background chick all the while she was posing as being part of the family. Melody was never supposed to find out about this relationship. the wool had been pulled over her eyes for ten years now and now she wanted to rise up, "dumb bitch" Toni said to himself as he laid there with his arm folded behind his head looking up at the signatures from inmates that had came and went on the bunk over his, Karen was elected queen bitch by the way she conducted herself by being there for ten years never letting the secret out. Toni being admirer of porn he had his own personal continual three-some and no one was the wiser. This was like a sex fantasy come true Karen was a real piece of work a jump off when ever Toni pulled her in the closet on her daily visit to the house and fucked her right under Melody's nose. That made Melody look bad in his eyes she was labeled as the ignorant one in the family. instead of queen bitch her birth right to be his queen bitch had been stripped unbeknown to her, he contemplated her end the ignorance that he claimed laid dormant inside of Melody brain was what he wanted to kill not her but the brain itself, He couldn't see her messing things up for him not now so he laid there and contemplated her death the plot would begin when the sentence had been passed down in court on the following day, the prison yard will be filled with gangsta's Toni knowing that his name was added to the list of ole timers "The Prison Greats" like a prison's hall of fame he knew he would find him a patsy to carry out the job to eliminate Melody; he laid there thinking about his upbringing and his parents philosophy every body wanted to be somebody was one of his father and mothers greatest sayings that when drug dealing took over his life reminiscing was the only way to kill the pain of a fifty five-year stretch and a murder plot this would become a project to Toni. The court room was packed with legal crew and teams from way back there to testify against Toni and the Social Service wanted to establish child support even though he couldn't get out until he became old with grey hair. This made him want the blood his first love Melody on his head even more knowing he couldn't control her any longer ate at him. He wanted his daughter's kidnapped and taken far away if the Social Service gave them back to her, he thought of a dozen ways where he could hurt, torture, kill, devalue, demote, and deface Melody until there was nothing left. The judge gave his verdict the sounds of freedom was muffled out and captivity was the corporate, the bailiff pulled his cuffs off the side of his waist ready to show the court room filled with strangers how tough he could be when putting them on big black thugs powerless to the system. Toni laughed as if he had gone insane in a matter of minutes he hawked and spit on the floor as the bailiff lugged him by the arm pass the judges' chambers.

"Fuck You!" Toni yelled while pulling his arm from the bailiff bucking for the front door knocking innocent victim out of the way as he shuffled his shackles across the hard marble floors. Every sheriff and bailiff in the court house took a dive all at the same time diving on top of Toni, the judge stood there with his mouth hanging open watching as the bailiff fought Toni and wrestled him into submission. Toni was just one of the familiar faces that passed through his court seemed like every week. He was tired to not throwing the book at them sooner. the State needed strong black African American males to work for them washing laundry, or shoveling shit, the best job the state could offer burying the dead. Toni knew this was a dumb move he was quickly rushed to the back of the jail house and stripped of his pride, he was thrown into solitary confinement this was perfect just what Toni wanted now he'd be able to plot the death and the money he would be willing to pay one of his fellow brothers to carry out the crime. The insurance policy he had on her had been establishing since the birth of his first born daughter. Seven million that's what his love to her was worth and now it was time to collect, fifty five years in prison for taking care of a woman that wouldn't even follow direction by hiding the yayo now he would be penalized for her fuck ups.

Her fuck up would be his down fall. Melody's name flowed through the prison yard and the fact that her ex- king pin boyfriend wanted her dead. The rewards would be sweet for a brother stepping out of prison ready to start a new life, he took application like a he was hiring at Burger king gangsta's and nigga's who wanted to be a true gangsta showed up to heed his call.

"So you think you have what it takes to be a true gangsta?" Toni asked each thug that stepped to his solitary confinement door the prison had decided he was a security risk and decided to leave him locked up in solitary confinement. Toni didn't let this stop

118

him. A big black thug walked up to his cell door asking for a description of the mark.

As if he was already hired for the job. Toni laughed.

"So you think you have what it takes to be a true gangsta, huh?" Toni asks as he peeped out the crack of paper that covered the window on his door to see the face of the nigga that approached his cell like a true hit man.

"I want this job and when you give it to me the job will be carried out." The thug said as he stood there waiting for a description of the mark he refused to let Toni gaze upon his face.

"She's my daughter's mother. I hate her and want her dead do you think you can do it, man?" Toni asks standing extra close to the door.

"If you don't mind me asking what did she do that have you on a mission to kill?" The thug asks with an intelligent look on his face.

"Why are you asking me question. I will pay you twenty gran to carry it out, so are we on?" Toni asks. "If so you can pick the money up at this address."

"When do you get out of here, man?' Toni asks.

"Tomorrow, man." The thug said while answering each question with honesty.

"Here's the address she probably still lurking around the house." Toni wrote down the address to his house not knowing Karen had moved in so quickly.

"And I also heard you wanted the kids too, am I right?" The thug asks.

"Of course, are you that heartless, man Toni answered answering his questions with a cold heart and a devilish grin?

The thug looked at him in the corner of the door shaking his head but the money Toni offered him was enough to set him pretty when he stepped foot out of those prison gates. He didn't want to murder no children but the money Toni offered spoke for itself. As did his character.

"Dirty dog." The thug said under his breath before leaving Toni's cell door.

Being a trustee he got to walk the prison hall's freely for being a trust worthy servant for the state for years. The day of the hit came and Melody had just left the Social Service office taking her girls back to the hotel room a stranger set her up in for a couple of days. She sat around upset that she hadn't enough money to take care of her girls no longer now that their father was out of their lives and she would be the single mother she always feared of becoming with no way of making ends meet, meanwhile her man of ten years was plotting on her and her children from behind prison gates.

The thug packed the remainder of his things from his white tee's, boxers, and socks including his tooth brush he had nothing to start over in society and the man would grant him nothing. On the way home from doing a ten year bid and being told what he could and couldn't do from strange men. Freedom was sweet. Before he could become truly free he would have to get the bulk of cash Toni promised him which was all illusion at this point in time after the job of taking out his woman of ten years was completed. The thug left the prison yard in a cab with his clothes wrapped in a sheet the state gave him. He traveled long and far to get to Toni's house; once he arrived he paid the cab his first and last dollar and hung around the neighborhood until melody was spotted or at least who he though was Melody. The woman he thought was Melody was Karen, she stepped out of her truck with little Toni on her hip as usual she grabbed grocery bags out of the back of her Lex truck Toni had brought her for fucking him behind his woman's back for ten years. She left her grocery on the porch one by one along with the baby he stood there patiently waiting for his mother. Karen turned around to grab

120

another bag to find a big black S&W gun pointed in her face her heart dropped to her stomach and swallowed hard thinking this was a trick of Melody's not being able to except the fact that Toni had another woman behind her back and in front of her face for ten years and she bared his first born son. Karen opened her mouth but words wouldn't come out, so she stood there not able to move as the bullets pour out of the chamber into her face.

"This is from Toni.' The thug said as he pulled the trigger of the gun and aimed and shot Karen and Toni first born son. He blew the trigger of the gun knowing he was about to receive a twenty gran for carrying out the crime. The money always talked while bullshit walked but he forgot in all his ten years in prison that a bird in the hand is better then two in a bush. Toni paced the floor of his five by ten cell knowing the news would reach him soon he planned on acting sad when in his cold heart he didn't care less, if this guy who claimed he was a hit man was a hit man the hit would been carried out by now with no problem Toni thought to himself as he wore out his white butter cookie sneakers walking back and forth. Count came and went he stood by his cell door as the corrections officer made his rounds counting each and every inmate in the institution he knew the message from the outside world would come he anticipated the hit. Laughing to himself over messing up Melody's life for her stupidity for not hiding the ya-yo like he told her too, her love meant nothing to him any more she was just a welfare chick he picked up and put up with for ten years of his life she was good for something opening and closing doors behind junkies when they came over to the house to cop some dope that was her job for ten years, and fucking him making her think he loved her when in all reality he didn't it was all about the money.

Melody and her five girls laid safe in the hotel watching television as the news came across the screen. She jumped off the bed and held her hands against her chest she couldn't believe the news she was hearing she watched on a cop arrested the man holding him down on the ground by force.

The house she lived in and raised her girls was splashed across the television screen with two bodies laid out covered in black plastic bags. Melody stood there wondering was that supposed to be her. She knew Toni told her he wanted her out she never imaged he would go to such lengths to get her and his daughters out of the house.

She packed up her daughters and headed south, the execution was document and Toni received a death sentence to go along with his fifty five years. Blinded by his love for money over his family and innocent blood of children.

Chapter 7

Ghetto Star Child

I remember her drifting away slowly but surely with each step as she walked down the block of Halsey Street. I was just a little girl who loved her mother more than life itself just like any other little girl. I sat there wondering would she come back but she never did. The son of man would have something to do with it as if he wasn't responsible for enough destruction already going on in the world. When she walked away she left an impression in my mind and heart like foot prints in the sand. As a child I felt fear, abandonment, she stripped me of any hopes of a bright future, being still a child herself Delfia the mother of Shane and Moe. She did what she seen a whole generation of teen mothers do she abandoned her babies because of lack she couldn't help it. The man had his foot in her back like he had it in the backs of so many others. I was a child borne into hope and once my mother abandoned me all hope faded away. When the streets called my mother she listened heeding its call. She became a product of street life prostitution, organized crime, and a variety of vices. I grew up not knowing her just remembering the pictures that played rapid in my mind like a movie projector.

My mother became consumed and lost in the crowd, lost in the party instead of being the life of it. Lost to addiction and co-dependency, lost in the alcoholism wanting to drink the adrenaline of night life these vices will eventually break a body down and maybe that's what it will take for her to come home to me.

"Ma was following her heart when she walked out on us." Moe said to her sista just one year under her 22 and 23 Shane being the baby.

"No, she wasn't. She was following the dope man." Shane blurted out letting out her steam.

"You think?" Moe said looking dead serious.

"He obviously made her feel more important than we did. She left us for him didn't she?" Shane replied.

"Don't worry the fake love affair she's having with crack is going to reveal itself sooner rather than later. Now look at me I'm following in her footsteps" Moe knowing her sista had been a pillow of strength for her through her addiction.

Moe was the head of this close knit family being the oldest at age 23 wasn't easy but she bared her load with a smile on her face and sometimes silent tears while wandering through the matrix called life. Her mother walked out leaving her with this title and a habit that developed much later in life, some body had to step up to the plate now a fully developed young woman Moe decided to go back to her old neighborhood on Halsey Street dead smack in the middle of Brooklyn, she stood there in front of an old deteriorating building checking out the rows of home that remained. As she reminisced about her and her sista's Shane's childhood and the last time they seen their mother walk

Down the block and turn the corner. This mirage took her mind all the way back in a matter of seconds like traveling in time and space. Each house held along with it special child hood memories from babies being born to somebody dying, Moe seen them come and go. She even saw them take dives out of twenty story building windows in the dead cold of winter carrying out suicidal thoughts. She stood in front of the house looking up at each window remembering how when she was a child gazing out of it like a sentinel waiting to see that familiar face come home once again. That when the picture of Delfia popped in her mind she remembered her mother standing at the stove making dinner and then "puff" she was gone. Moe held her head down with tears running down her cheeks she wondered why would her mother do this to her? It was a feeling that was hard to shake. And why should she spend the next forty years of her life wondering though the wilderness of life? She wondered why couldn't her life at least one parent in it? She prayed that the curse that enveloped itself in and out of her life since her conception would finally be lifted. She wondered why was this placed on her and her sista's head and at what price? And why was she being punished for being borne and than she realized that her mother was born under the same generational curse as she. Vulnerable to street life and open for suggestions including the elements called pimps, hustlers, and suga daddies, skeptics and crooks and all other vices and vapors affiliated.

Moe stood there trying to build up the strength and confidence to move forward just thinking about it made her weak." How can a person resist street life? When it's all around them." Moe thought to herself as she sat there on the step. The ghetto was like a mother to her raising her making her put on a variety of mask in order to fit in and survive. Moe's heart melted as she thought about the world of problems she and her sista's been through from being molested and not telling to being abused by men they thought loved them. Leaving her sista Shane with these men's seed to raise all alone in the middle of ghetto life where only the fit survive. Moe never once considered having children her heart was set on much bigger things even with limited resources. Moe never knew that events from her past would map out her future. She exploded with anger and it wasn't hard for the people walking down the side walk to tell she was one of the lost one's. Born at a time when being born lost was a trend instead of a human condition. After twenty three years of let downs, set backs, pull-outs, disagreements, and disappearing acts. This affected Moe's personality and the fact that Delfia abandoned her this left a lasting affect on her development in life and the game of life, no-one understood her pain, the only way Moe knew to cover it up was to act it out by walking in her mother's footsteps. Moe knew she had been dealt a faulty hand in life and no-one gave a fuck!

All the while.

Fate smiled on Shane delivering each and every prayer she prayed in her lap on the regular.

"Fuck!" Moe yelled as she grabbed hands full of hair burying her face in the palms of her hands, luckily Halsey Street was deteriorating and the buildings abandoned because she needed a place to stay. Walking the street for hours at a time while stuck in a time warp.

Shane's house was an occasional resting place. She sat there on the step until she seen the sun go down. she had to find away inside of the house when she crawled in an opened window she noticed the house was cold, damp, and musty, there was no doubt its inhabitance was rat infested but they would be tolerable considering her situation.

She planned on not walking the streets on this night for fear of being seen by a drug dealer she owned a pretty penny. He was on the look out for her, himself being a cracked addicted made matters even worst. She shivered as she sat there in the corner mad because she couldn't go back to her sista Shane's house for fear of putting each and very body that lived there in danger meaning the children. She cover up to keep warm with an old blanket she found thrown over a box filled with old paint chips.

"Why?" Moe asks thinking about how she needed a mother or father at times like these but never had one. She was like a lost child inside that refused to grow up. She sat there in the dark listening to sounds of street life all around her this never seemed to cease no matter of how bad a fall a brother or sista had going on in their lives. The game was still being played. the sound of trash being kicked around scared Moe she stepped up to investigate as she walked to the back window she seen another female with her back pinned against the side of the house while a john did what ever he wanted to do from the front, Moe stood there like a voyeur until the sexual act that was being performed was finished.

"Damn." Moe said to herself as she seen the prostitute with the hard New York accent snatch her money from the young black punk she considered as a client.

"Excuse me!" The prostitute said as she pushed the guy back and stumbled over loose dry wall laying in the way she looked over at the window and seen Moe watching. She laughed as she bends down to pick up her pair of thongs that laid near by on the ground slipping back into them.

"I think we have ourselves a voyeur." The hooker said as she walked over to the big medal door pushing it open, Moe walked over and moved the clutter out of the way opening the door all the way.

"What's your name? Sweetie. The hooker asks Moe when she seen it was a woman watching not a man.

"Moe!" she said in a loud hard tone trying to sound hard after just finishing a good cry.

"Did you know your trespassing?" the hooker announced.

"I grew up in this house so you're the one trespassing." Moe announced in return as she stood there look rough dressed like a dike.

The hooker pulled out her money she had accumulated through out the day counting it before stuffing it in a piece of toilet paper and then in her pussy. Moe became extremely loud as if she was ready

127

to battle if it came down to that. She refused to back down.

"Honey, I was here first!" The crack addicted hooker revealed as she pulled a razor out of her French roll.

Moe backed up.

"Hey, listen up I'm going over here and what you do over here is your business, this house is big enough for me to hide in and for you to turn your tricks in. I see you make a pretty penny too." Moe said as she took another step forward she was willing to fight to get what she wanted if that's what it took. She knew she could take this prostitute down if that's what shit boiled down too and she would.

"I'm not dividing nothing! Not with you anyway boo my man wouldn't like that." The hooker screamed then the shakes begin to take over the doe eyed hooker's body. she reached in her raggedy bra pulling her works out, Moe stood there wanting to participate in the activities she watched on as the hooker hyped up her ripped up red dress and started skin poppin, she revealed all her flesh wounds that bear a ugly sight she loved to pop her heroin it made the rush turn her on mind, body, and soul. Dark ugly circles inhabited her flesh bearing the face of her past or present pain her demons were bad, Moe could tell the elements had taken over her whole existence just as they had hers. As she watched the hooker she wondered could this prostitute be her mother or if her mother was living this same type of lifestyle somewhere in New York? Moe backed up making her way back to the corner of the room to cop a squat and watch this unknown hooker go through the motion. She cover herself to try to keep warm because the chills were beginning to haunt her flesh as well she wished for a hit of crack the drug that was destroying her life as she walked the same path her mother trotted.

The hooker stood there lost and turned out frozen in her steps unable to move. The heroin had taken over all rules of reason at least this is the message that reached her brain.

This is the product and power of the same demon that took her mother by the hand and walked her out of Moe and Shane's lives. The hooker stood there drooling all over the front of her red dress while the cigarette she held burned a hole in her flesh. Moe scratched her flesh uncontrollably as she sat there then the front door of the residence opened as a tall black man dressed like as pimp walked in. he was very distinguished in the way he walked. Moe knew trouble was about to erupt. She sat there silent hoping not to be discovered. The blanket she held was pulled over her head not wanting to see what was about to happen. The hooker never saw it coming. The pimp took his fist without saying a word hitting the hooker in the face without reason, taking both his hands he tugged her panties off throwing them to the side then he took his finger pulling the tissue filled with money out of her privates, before he left he took his foot and kicked her in the side like a animal he had no remorse for a woman and it showed in his treatment of them.

The hooker laid there in pain knowing not to talk or make eye contact with her pimp he had her on strict codes and talking could have been her death with out remorse.

"Stop hitting her!" Moe yelled not being able to remain silent any longer she seen her mother go through this same type of abuse and she always went back to her abuser more in love after he beat her down then she was before the abuse started. Moe had a hate for abusive men because she would have to learn to tolerate this for the protection she seeked.

"Do you want some little mama?" the pimp asks as he walked in her direction scaring the shit out of Moe.

"Who let you in here?" he asked standing there in front of her looking like a tower of strength. He took the cover throwing it to the side before pulling her blouse open looking at her breast, Moe stood there looking young and tender underneath the dirt and grim that covered her face. He took both his pointer fingers running them along the tip of her nipples as if he was measuring them.

"What's your name sweet thing?" He asked as he looked her down from head to toe past the diked out gear, he seen money making possibilities.

She knew she couldn't run out the door from fear of being seen by the crack head drug dealer who vowed to burn her with gasoline if he seen her on the streets, so she stood there like a little child who was following in her mothers footsteps all the bad things became easy to live. This was a part of the generational curse that plagued not just her but millions. She viewed her own life as one big mishap after the other never seeming to end it was like walking through a labyrinth looking for an exit while running into big bad wolves with each and every twist and turn. This brought on immediate flash backs of the man her mother use to live with her mind went to Halsey Street in its younger years when she was six and Shane five. she remembered how the continual beatings her mother received made her cringe while lying in bed at night listening to the fights and cursing and waking up to holes in the walls in the morning and how the man that told her mother he loved her would beat her black and blue like clock work afterwards telling her he loved her using her like a slave. The pimp had no clue what situations ran through her heart as well as her veins this was a part of the make up that made Moe the person she was and there was no changing this dogs old spots she went off swinging at the pimp he caught her hands before her fist landing in his face.

"Hold up little mama, what's wrong with you! Are you crazy or just shell shocked?" He held on to her hands as she tried to break free but there was no controlling this led pipe grip. He held her until she understood that he was man and she was woman.

Moe popped out of the haze that was fogging her mind that led to the flash back she broke out in a cold sweat.

"Damn, girl you got it bad." The pimp said scare to let her go himself.

The hooker made her way past the excitement and ran out the door before the wrath of kon returned in her direction.

"You never answered my question." The pimp asks Moe.

"My name is Moe short for Mo-tae" she said as she calmed down.

Meanwhile...

Shane was the baby in the family. She had children that made her feel alive and they kept her alive for longer than she wished. These babies were the way she replaced her mother's love that had been snatched out of her life at such a juvenile age. She day dreamt a lot about becoming the star her mother would have been proud of. But never had the courage to actually make her dreams come true she was the mother of two girls whose fathers all abandoned their seed just as her mother did. They all turned the other cheek instead of acknowledging their children this came as no surprise in the ghetto to a man especially if he felt he didn't have the resources to take care of the seed they planted in the young innocent not fully grow girls that got pregnant. Shane had her own way of dealing with the dysfunctional life that she was drop into she would write down all the pain she felt on the regular turning adversity into music. She sat in a dark corner of the house as her daughters slept writing all the feeling she felt about her mother and the men that tried to destroy her being like monsters. This brought on strong crying spells. She picked up a piece of tissue and wiped her eyes not knowing why she was being led to do half of the things she had done in her twenty two years of being on the planet. Her mother never been there for her not like she was supposed too she hadn't a clue about being a good mother she just played it by ear like all the other young single black mothers burdened by the generational curse of being alone to raise children. The words to the song she wrote as she sat there lit up the page it made her feel each and every situation she wrote down memories flooded her mind of the things her and her sista been through all the life changing experiences. She knew Moe was a drug addicted but she didn't know what to say to make her stop using. Her taking drugs were making her do crazy things that seemed to land her in jail. She feared her sista' life was in danger once again. She wanted to help her but had not a clue how too so she just prayed. This became a part of the song she wrote everything she wrote down flowed and made a hell of a lot of sense, the words made her cry even harder as she thought about the walk her mother was on and if she was dead or alive ate at her heart all of her life and there was no way of finding out especially when the rode she already traveled was extremely hard and long. The system has made her want to take herself out on many occasion but her children was the angels that kept this feeling from taking place. She sat there and drifted off to sleep as she had a sweet dream about her mother and sista Moe riding in the back of a limo she was zapped immediately to a stage where she was performing and the crowd loved her.

She was being praised for the affect the music she wrote touched woman lives as well as men. This dream felt so real she didn't want to wake up the dream immediately turned into a night mare she seen

Moe break free from the concert and take off running for her life in the dream and a dark figure lurk in the shadows behind her. Shane laid there as her eyeballs moved back and forth in her head; she moved from side to side watching her sista run in this dream before awaking she seen Moe fall into a big swirl of quick sand, and this woke her up.

She jumped up and ran over to the front door to go outside and stand on the front porch of her apartment building looking up and down the streets at all the drug action taking place, she lived dead smack in the middle of Brooklyn, New York's Pacific Avenue her sista was famous for standing on corners pan handling in the neighborhood. She knew her sista's was doing everything she could to help her all of her life but the burdens and help from people started slacking off this made Moe slip and her slipping turned into a full blow mental problem. She took to the streets looking for the woman who called herself Ma. She looked in all five boroughs Brooklyn, Queens, Staten Island, Manhattan, and Coney Island looking but never finding her. After age twelve Moe took to the streets on the search. She promised her sista Shane when she returned she would come back with her mother on her arm instead she did the same disappearing act, coming back months later turned out on heroin, crack, and anything that cover pain. If she was in pain drugs were everywhere to help her cover up the great pain that felt as if it would kill her eventually.

Moe resistance broke her down as always she left with the pimp after he promised her he would protect her from the drug fiend dealer that promised to kill her on sight once she explained her story to him. She believed each sweet line he dropped in her ear; he promised her a place to stay along with fresh food to eat when ever she got hungry. This was enough to make a lost puppy follow him as he walked to his pink Rose Royce that he parked in front of the house Moe grew up in, sex was a part of the deal as if she didn't know this before making the decision to ride off into the sunset with him leaned to the side as he drove down the street he sped past all the night life to get his new find home as quickly as possible to start his training process like going through junior college. She would be a pimp's prize. Moe sat there not caring about much of nothing her feelings had been numbed from the lack of love and this was the replacement for her mother leaving her for twenty three years ago, the men who she chose over Moe and Shane popped into Moe's mind and how her mother would believe a man over her children and how her mother always put her abuser up on a pedestal, making them dinner whenever he came home from work and rubbing his feet after he kicked off his boots, just the thought made her sick.

"Stop the car!" Moe yelled before attempting to get out.

"Hold up!" The pimp said as he reached for her arm.

Moe opened the door handle and stuck one foot out of the Rose Royce.

"Are you flippin out on me again?" the pimp asks as he held on to her arm. He could see she had a real full blown mental problem.

Moe took one more look at him and changed her mind; his sweet face melted her heart along with her pussy. This was a feeling she wasn't use to being a man hater from birth; she never had the chance to get close from fear of being abused like her mother.

"Calm down and get back in the rose." The pimp knew he had a walking time bomb on his hand and once he set the rules to the game into affect there was no turning back. She would be made to know this if it took abusive methods to lay down the law.

"Why did you want to go and open the door?" The pimp asks.

Moe laughed.

134

"Exactly what is it that makes you do the things you do? I'm just curious. When you went off on me at the abandon house I thought you would pull out a gun and blow my head off." The pimp said.

"I'm just been going through a lot like all of my life that's all." Moe said in a sarcastic voice not knowing the stranger in which she chose to confide in.

The pimp looked over at her wondering what nigga got his hands on her first to make her into such a monster like she appeared to be. Instead of a money making flower like she was supposed to be. If by choice she decided she wanted to represent his stable along with all the other woman whose self esteem drove them to come to him looking for a father figure to protect them. Showing them a better way then the life they lived all their lives, he had to break them down to make sure they seen the same picture he seen if they didn't see the same thing he did. He would make them see it. That was a number one rule never make a person do what they didn't want to do. After all the corporate pimps that ran America never made a person do what they didn't want too, so why should a street pimp? A Corporate pimp give you what you need and want for a price and so do a pussy selling pimp you need pussy you want pussy, Freddy fed his pimp sociology to Moe like food as she sat there looking at him from the corner of her eyes not trusting the ground he walked on. He explained to her he would show her all the things no body else would. he would be the one to show her how the world is ran inside out and he explained what he wanted from her in return. Freddy was smooth sitting there with his extra big platinum pinky ring filled with diamonds as he rode down the blocks of Brooklyn Flatbush in his light pink Rose Royce with the zebra interior. He explained to her that he was borne a pimp and planned on dying a pimp it was a part of his nature and no one could take this away from him. This being his birth right in life. If Moe was hungry to live she

135

will be willing to come join his stable and make all the money she could while the money in the

Streets was ripe and flowing his management skills would help her to manage it all putting thing in her broken life in prospective. To heal from her mother abandoning her. He knew he was talking to an abused woman's child who also was abused and a walking time bomb waiting to explode. He could see Moe was still a little girl at heart by the way she talked and held a conversation. The stable he ran was full of abused product and damaged goods very rarely a diamond in the rough walked through the pussy palace's doors. Freddy was also into the cleaning up and turning them out business replacing the soul of the lost into the soul of the found his stable ranged from rape victims, to incest victims, to the woman who never learned how to love herself and she needed to be filled with love from a man who was like a father figure to this type of woman giving a man all her money would buy her love, The sex addicted love addicts looking for continual co- dependency from whom ever and what ever they could this meaning dope. In order for these women to feel complete they all felt they had to buy their self worth by turning a pretty penny hustling day in and day out for the man who made them feel complete and whole like no other pimp. He ruled their soul replacing their damaged childhoods with smoked glass and blinders with hopes and promises of a good times and money.

"Cars, I love clothes and cars and money." Freddy's conversation went in a whole other direction. "Clothes are my weakness you want to make me fuck you? Come in my house bearing gifts of bright colored suits by the top of the line designers and let's not forget they better be tailor made." Freddy said as he cruised the Parkway as his car reached one of the many corners he controlled his ho's that stood on post all held their heads down not eyeballing him for fear of being in violation of one of his many strict rules and violation meant being strip of your pride as well as your woman hood in public places.

"So why did you want to be a pimp" Moe asks anticipating the answer.

"I can't reveal because I'm in a clique ruled by pimps and if I told you the answer to that question I would be in violation of my number one rule, this game is not being carried out for me it's for you, baby." Freddy said.

Freddy pulled up in a neighborhood where hooker ran rapid they walked the block wearing thongs, with bra's some had their asses exposed with tattooed of x-rated poses and roses with guns. Cars pulled up like they were visiting Santa's work shop this was the corner of pussy negotiations and contracts signed in paid in blowjobs, anal sexual acts was a big pay off as well as the fore play freaks rode through in disguises some just rode by to take a look at what was becoming of their neighborhoods such as church vans, and truckers ready to spend money for a hooker to make them feel like a real man, money was flowing like milk and honey in the valley of the dolls. The police even bought pussy on the DL faking arrest on the regular having twisted controlled sexual acts they performed undercover Moe had seen this like everyday on her journey's this pimp wasn't telling her nothing she hadn't seen or done before she just never considered a pimp for protection or to finesse her like Freddy's tongue he was a sure enough version of a Super pimp from the ole school he had to study her to figure out the diagnosis for her full blown mental problem. She watched a real live violation in action as the Rose Royce came to a slow cruise than a complete stop on the corner of Atlantic Avenue in Brooklyn. Freddy stepped out the car flier than ever pimpin as he walked with confidence and approached one of his ho's eyeballing him as he pulled up in the car that blew his ego up, he back slapped his ho in front of all the people on the street and stripped her of all her jewelry and money as a form of punishment. She didn't say a word of back talk. She just grin and bared it like she was trained to do in order to prevent any further abuse.

"Damn." Moe said as she could feel the slap. She grabbed her face while sitting there watching from the Rose Royce window slumped down in her seat she laughed as if it was funny. Freddy got back in the Rose and sped off he was in a daze the conversation stopped for mediation purposes had taken its place and silence was necessary.

Society viewed Freddy's kind as the scum of the earth for the work he did like an angel of death turning out young girl and watching them deteriorate before his eyes not caring about their well being just the money. If they could have shot him down in the street he would have been dead a long time ago. But how could one pimp persecute the other? He started pulling young tender pussy's to exploit and sell on the world wide meat market in his early twenties it sold like fresh exotic fish. He started on the block he lived on Utica Avenue up the hill in Brooklyn. He sold his neighbor daughters virginity to a boy he knew and when he made his first dollar shit went through the roof like on the stock exchange pussy became a commodity item like coffee and tea worth fighting for it could be brought and sold to the highest bidder. He seen himself graduating to another level wearing the fliest suits from K-marts to top of the line Armani, Cole Haan, Johnston and Murphy, Brooks Brothers and of course Gucci in some of the brightest colors to impress the ho's that he managed in the stable he ran that was what life was all about and he loved it. Everyday hustling pussy became king in the streets. Hustling and grinding was what he woke up and laid down to this gave him life. His stable were filled with white ho's it wasn't that Freddy was prejudice against his own kind, he was just a enterprising man out to make money and white ho's was marketable in the neighborhoods, he ran more whites than black one at least in his eyes but black pussy always out shined the white pussy like super stars because of the exoticness of it in the eyes of men. Moe would be the only black face in this stable if she chose to be. She craved the attention Freddy offered her along with the protection. She would be finally treated like a true woman and be loved what else was there as far as she was concerned after all that is the reason her mother left her so she figured why not try it too. Freddy tried to take it light when it came to the abuse of his girl but if they tipped the scale of justice in his present there wasn't no telling what would happen.

"My mother left me for a man like you; she left me and my sista Shane to fin for ourselves in an empty house with no furniture and the lights cut out. If it weren't for my grandmother helping us to survive until she passed away there is no telling where we would have ended up." Moe exposed her life story as she looked straight ahead not eyeballing him as she talked. Freddy looked in her direction he knew at that very moment in time he had Moe she would be his and all by her own choosing. confessing to him "the sin of the mother" this was the testimony his ears been waiting for and the hook happened before he even reached the house she brought his pitch he knew he had the knack for charm he held a PHD in pitching to the ladies and he knew how to make them see the dream and believe it.

"So, where is your mother now?" Freddy asks already knowing the answer to the question. Her answer wouldn't be much different then the ho's that came before her. Because she was born and raised in the ghetto Freddy heard all kinds of confessions from girls sleeping with the mothers husbands and getting kicked out by their mothers to live on the streets, to the stories about the girls who been raped by an uncle to being abused by their own flesh and blood fathers confession period of the game wasn't pretty trying to play preacher to the tenderoni's and father to the molested who still wanted daddy touch this perverted world of sexual pleasure when it folds would take along with it the souls of the twisted and lost souls of the hurt and crushed.

"This game never stops, baby." Freddy explained as he pulled up in the drive way of his sex palace he called heaven.

"I bet with you in it.' Moe said as she stepped out the rose Royce.

"All the ho's in my house will be stark raving mad when I step in the door with you on my arm, just cover your ears ignored them." Freddy knowing how he loved excitement.

Freddy's game was tight, he changed his life from the depressing economic madness when black men where considered ill willed back in the days because of lack of employment and limited education. Insecurity concerning his economic power and turned the kingdom he was manufacturing here on earth turning it into the Con- Edison of the ghetto. He drew money from north, south, east, and west refusing to be pimped by a woman in fear of being called a "sucker" tagged and labeled across his forehead, he picked the poorest neighborhood in Brooklyn to have a house built from the ground up naming it "The Pussy Palace" he took extra special care in picking out his ho's watching carefully before pursuing them. He would lay his smooth tongue at their feet licking them from head to toe with his rap like the snake he was. He had to make them see the same dream he seen in order for them to feel where he was coming from and the role he could play in their lives. They would have to want the same thing he wanted in life this would open the door. He knew how the woman's anatomy worked and knew how woman sat around thinking about romantic love twenty four hours a day this is where he went wrong with Moe.

"So you say your mother abandoned you?" Freddy asks trying to hurt her feelings before he pitch the rap that would take her over.

"I never got to know my mother but when I hit the streets my intentions was to find her and ask her why she abandoned me and my sista?" Moe's confession started again.

"So, you do have family, where's your sista." He asks waiting for names and addresses something to use for future resources.

"My sista name is Shane." Moe answered wanting to protect Shane and her babies. Since he was offering to protect her from the crack head drug dealer she wanted protection for her family as well in order to get what he wanted.

"I rather not talk about her!" Moe said raising her voice Freddy touched a nerve but she had to do what she had to do for protection if it meant tricking for the protection then tricking it would be.

"Why don't you want me to meet your sista?" Freddy ask standing there looking like super fly.

"Because I rather leave her out of this." Moe yelled.

Freddy unlocked the door of the Pussy Palace opening it wide as him and Moe walked inside.

"So what kind of pimp do you consider yourself to be?" Moe asks because she had seen them all. She let him have his fun pitching while she listened but he wasn't telling her nothing she hadn't heard before in her twenty three years she been with and knew a variety of pimps but never had one offer to protector from her demons.

"I'm no sense kind of pimp that don't take no bullshit. You see, I know who I am, I'm not like the young punk taken the streets today ain't nobody stopping my flow you best be believing that, I'm from the old school, these want to be gangsta's liven life on the reckless side beating, robbing, and killing each other like there's no tomorrow just like the man want

141

them to do. They done adapted some shit the Italian taught them from all the gangsta's movie that was being played when those nigga's was babies in the damn crib now everybody's in search of an identity after the identity has been established the cops is on stand by waiting for a nigga to fuck up so they can lock them up the more they think their gangsta'a the more jails and prison will be built and funeral homes mind you. Maybe that's what happened to your mother she probably found a man that treat her like a woman with a fake identity and his breakdown of the way shit really is in America drove both their asses to the streets.

Moe listened she calculated what she wanted to do if she wanted to remain there or not or take back to the streets scared of her shadow in fear of being killed, Milo the cracked out drug dealer walked the streets religiously looking for her he had a vendetta and it was going to be carried out because that is the thought he had buried in his mind and held on to it like buried treasure. He held on to a gallon of gasoline that he vowed to burn her or her house down, this was the mission he was on and Moe knew it. He planned on burning her to a crisp if he caught up with Moe Brooklyn wasn't big enough for the both of them one of them would have to leave in order to survive. Freddy pitch to Moe for half the night he wanted her to choose him to be her man, he figure she was as weak as they come when in all reality the streets made a woman like her strong and weak for the vice and illusions that surrounded her on the daily basis. He displayed the fruits of his labor well he wore a big diamond pinky ring that he promised he would knock a bitch out if she disrespected him in any way including reckless eye contact.

Moe stood there in the middle of the floor and revealed her self fully to Freddy she was confirming his protection to her.

"That's what I'm talking about, baby." Freddy said as he sat gangsta style in his big wooden freak chair this was the money making chair in his pussy palace, he watched on as Moe freaked herself standing there in the middle of the floor.

"I didn't even see all this coming.' Freddy said as he stroked his chin with his long pointy fingers he was real pimp there was no doubt about this any woman who picked her man right would have picked him over all the pimps on the market displaying their qualities and marketing skills along with their Christmas list of brand new Cadillac's, Custom made quality suits in a rainbow assortment of colors. Electrifying the mind and thought patterns of a ho. This is the game marketing, distributing, delivery, pitching, and packaging, if the ho's didn't look good the money wouldn't flow, if the pimp didn't look good and successful he could sell himself like a ho, delivering the ho's to the johns this process was one big open market place and cycle and the money was dynamite in Freddy's eyes. Every player out there even the female pimps that joined the ranks of this game wanted to get paid living lavish lifestyle off the freaky feelings of others.

Moe moved as if she was riding an invisible pole in the middle of his pussy palace floor like a porn star. She didn't care how she looked or smelled she flashed pussy all over the place like she knew pimps like, marketing her moves and displaying her abilities. She needed this man's protection for her nieces and her sista and if riding a pole proves that then she would continue to ride.

"Damn!" Freddy said making her want to cover up but she didn't she continued to dance and move to the slow sexy music that left the room spinning with colors like at the end of a rainbow.

"Will you protect me?" Moe asks as she walked over to Freddy and stood in front of him she took her finger and ran them across her own nipples like he did when he seen her in the abandoned house. He stared for a minute surprised at the sudden transformation.

"Protect you... Done." Freddy said as he took the floor and handed her the clothes she had strolled all over the living room before his other ho's walked in. He had what he wanted now it was time to make money.

In the ghetto unwanted children were all over the place as far as Freddy was concerned he knew his life being spent as one that is another reason he figured he could Mack, bringing in all the low self esteem woman and woman with unstable personalities that think in order to be loved and liked the female sex organ could and would give them all the things they ever wanted in life, all the while expressing and displaying the jealousy that layed beneath there skins taking out there hate and revenge on each other like a pack of hungry wolves. Freddy graced his woman hoping they would never decide to go with another pimp in order to establish this he would have to take drastic measures in making sure his girl didn't approach another.

Milo found the house as Moe was way on the other side of town he seen lights on and walked up to the front porch door turned the door knob hoping to just walk in and ambush Moe and her family. He knocked standing at the front door looking like a bonified crack fiend. He knocked again there was no answer.

"Hello, Moe get out here!" He yelled.

The door flew open.

"Moe's not here, get off my porch!" Shane yelled as her babies in the back ground started cry.

"I need my money!" he shouted as he tried to push the door and just walk in to see if Moe was home his self.

"I said she's not here, she doesn't live here anymore." Shane said before taking her hand and

144

pushing the cracked out of control fiend away from her front door.

The can of gasoline Milo hid on the side of the house. His plan to burn the bitch out if she didn't give him the twenty dollars she owed him that night. A fire would be set. He waited patiently like he did for the last three month for his twenty dollar. he copped a squat on the side of the house in the cut where he wouldn't be seen he had no feelings any more crack had him feeling like a lost animal in the streets like all the other crack fiend that is what society wanted to see or they wouldn't have put crack out here to destroy innocent lives. There is obviously an execution and the dope heads are the prey.

Shane put her babies to bed and read the girl a bed time story and prayed before the lights went out in their room, Shane did her normal she sat in the dark corner that was like a meditation spot and started to write but this time not a song, she decided after much

Research to write one of the many record company executives she had been told to call by girls at her job McDonalds. She sung for them and they loved her this was a inheritance that some hated on her for because she possessed a quality that they didn't. She put the letter in a big yellow envelope sitting it on the table by the front door so she could mail it the next morning, she prayed for Moe and her mother before drifting off to sleep. Milo knew all was well he crept around the house pouring large amounts of gasoline. He just knew Moe was in the house not caring who else was there. He took out his lighter and put the dime piece of crack on the tip of his stem. He pulled until his gut felt like they would pop out of his being. Once he released the smoke that he almost choked off he took his lighter and lit the circle of gas that surrounded the house. The flames were so intense he caught his shirt on fire he started to run and scream before him dropping and rollout into the streets. He landed on his feet unscratched as smoke rose higher than the house Shane smelled the smoke in her sleep it was over powering her little girls where on the upper level of the house. The fire was so intense she couldn't get to them. she screamed until her voice reached the upper level of the house hoping her older daughter would here her but she didn't, the girl slept the whole time not knowing the house was on fire. Shane ran out into the streets screaming for help as her neighbors in the hood she lived in heard her voice they came to assist as much as they could until the fire department arrived. Shane passed out as the bodies of her little girl were in the fire set by a crack head on a mission. Shane was taken into the ambulance as the fire was put out and small body bags rolled past her. She thought she would die her babies where gone and it was all because of Moe and her drug habit and street debts.

Moe' soul was not her own as of this moment Freddy had to do his job she would be broke down and turned all the way-out he wasn't going to let this commodity item walk out no not now she showed him and chose him he was the king of the pussy palace not no other, ho's wasn't allowed to explore that's why the break down was so important dedication and devotion, protection and guidance, like husband and wife. He wasn't willing to let none of those female pimps get there hands on none of his ho's either promising to eat pussy to reel them in. money was the name of this game. The world couldn't run without it neither could the pussy palace. He named all the white girls that belonged to his stable names like the zodiac, Scorpio walked in the door bearing a suit in a long plastic bag straight from Gucci.

"This is for you, baby." Scorpio said as she check Moe out she never seen Freddy bring a colored girl home before. This was some new shit. White meat ruled this pussy palace she figured something was wrong financially.

"You alright baby?" Scorpio asks as she looked over at Moe wondering why she was there.

She knew white girls had Freddy gone. Their pussy was like gold to him. He could make a white girl do what ever he wanted her too from eating ass to sucking balls while he talked on the phone, Scorpio knew something was definitely out of place in this white pussy palace. Moe would have to go she wasn't getting Scorpio's pimp.

"So Moe where are you from, baby?' Scorpio asks as she propped her white flesh on the black leather couch her body was beautiful like milk no scratches just beauty from head to toe.

Shane's world had been snatched out from under her, her baby 's were gone and there was no bringing them back, the ambulance drivers and fire men consoled her apologizing for the tragedy that had just taken place. She clutched on to the big yellow envelope with the song she wrote inside that she' no idea would eventually change her life forever. She went through a long process of getting her thoughts together after the tragic fire and the lost of her children. Months passed by she hadn't seen Moe or knew where she might have been, Shane wondered aimlessly wondering where her sista was so she could tell her what happened while she was gone. She had done a disappearing act like her mother, Shane lived in shelter after shelter sometimes she found her self walking the streets of Brooklyn with head hanging down in deep depression wishing life would get better but some how it always ended up getting worst. Shane hoped to see her sista's face in the crowd of pedestrians that flooded the sidewalk as she walked down the street. She prayed that deep down inside for change hoping god heard her prayers, she asks to be heard this one time in life because with the current condition that she was living under it felt as if the walls would close in on her.

Shane stood there looking up to heaven with both her arms stretched as if she would reach right through the sky.

"Just this one time, god!" Shane yelled with her arms stretched out to the heavens.

Pictures of her little girls popped into her mind along with a picture of Milo and the reason he came to the house that night it was like the heaven was talking to her in the middle of Brooklyn. Shane put two and two together in her mind before she screamed to the top of her lungs. As people who watched she was just another New Yorker gone crazy they walked along as if this was normal not caring or trying to find out what the problem was. Moe was in the clique now Freddy let her in his little family called the "stable" she turned her tricks harassing her johns for money after she slept with them, men who picked her up wished they never did because of her insane demeanor. She con-ed and harassed men being the man hater that had to sell pussy in order to survive, while out tricking she ran into an older black woman who looked all used up and her body broke down. But she was so hypnotized by street life not much else mattered. This hookers demons were much worst than the skin popper heroin had taken over their body's like the body snatchers. The unknown hooker nodded out in between sentences.

"Where you goin." The ho asks Moe. Peeping out of one eye while the other one was shut.

Moe felt a special connection with this middle aged hooker she stood there on post in the cold of winter wearing a thong that was dingy and an over coat that she let remain hanging open and high heel shoes with plastic clear heels.

"What's your name?" Moe asks as she checked out the older hookers moves. She never said a word she just stood there nodding out higher than words could express; her last john had put her on, a car pulled up.

"What's your name?" Moe asks again.

"Delia, damn it!" she shouted in Moe's direction Moe's mouth fell open she was finally standing face to face with her mother. The lady that left her and her sista for the streets life immediately turned into the seven year old child in her heart standing in Delpia's presents. She didn't even recognize her own daughter she was so far gone. The streets in its hard activity had chewed her up and spit her out like a bad taste. There was nothing drugs that turned her into a hard core junkie that was on a continual mission without end Delpia sold her body since she was old enough to fuck and did heroin, crack, meth, marijuana, and any thing that was flammable or made smoke.

She left her two beautiful children for a man that never cared for her and wished her harm once he used her up and sat her out. Prison was like a home since she didn't have one.

Moe grabbed her mother and hugged as tight as she could not wanting to ever let her out of her sight again but she would give in, she shrugged her shoulders and pushed her away.

"Get off me! What you doin!" Delpia asks as she reached in her purse pulling out an old can of mace to spray Moe in the face. She figures she was another hooker trying to steal her post and being defensive was the only way to remedy the problem.

"It's me momma, Moe!" she yelled to the top of her lung in the middle of the street trying to prevent her mother from walking to a tricks car that had just pulled up to the curb. Moe had big rain drop tears running down her face as she tried with all her heart to capture her mother's memory back like it use to be.

"Momma, I'm not your mother trick who are you and what do you want?" Delia asks looking dead serious in the face. Her eyes were full of cold and her skin dried out and ashy from her abuse and drug usage. She scratched her self uncontrollably.

"I'm your daughter how could you forget me and Shane, momma!" Moe cried with her hands on her mothers arm shoulders pulling her towards her to hold never wanting to let her out of her sight ever again.

"I was hoping I would find you and now you're here." Moe said as she didn't want to let her mother out of her sight ever again. Moe's mother raged. She didn't want to remember her or Shane. she hadn't idea she had grand kids all her body subliminal messages was telling her to follow the demon that made her leave in the first place which was a demon named heroin and crack. Moe and Shane couldn't make her come around if they tried.

Moe sat on the curb and cried like a baby as she watched a car pull and Delphi got in it never once looking back but shooting up as she rode off into the sunset.

Shane received a letter when she walked over to the local post office to get her mail. The letter she received explained that the cd she sent out to be reviewed was hot and she was wanted by the record company they wanted her to come in and sign a contract with promises of stardom.

"What's stardom without my little girls, sista, and mother, to share it with? She balled the letter up and turned to the streets following in those same footsteps that seemed to become a family tradition. She never saw Moe or her mother again. Not recognizing the blessing she had just prayed for handed to her on a silver platter. The subliminal same subliminal message grabbed her by the hand carrying her into the unknown.

Chapter 8

Pee Wee's Pair of Dice

The dice crashed against the cement wall "6 when she stops!" Pee Wee along with everybody else as the bloated dices landed. All the inmates stood by the doorway looking for the C.O to appear before count. This was one of many games Pee Wee mastered rolling dice it was like he was born with a pair of dice carved in the palm of his hand. Cards were another one of the games Pee Wee mastered three cards Monte the game of masters he'd always say. "The black will set you back while the red will put you ahead" Peewee announced not knowing this game had been phased out on the streets ever since his incarceration. After the games came to an rowdy end each inmate paid up with nasty hard looks on their faces. This was all they knew for recreation and Pee Wee would be the one to give it to them like the master of ceremonies creating illusion and killing time.

Cigarettes, candy bars, clothes and chicken flowed like water in Pee Wee's direction for the whole time he was down and swolls his meal of choice. He stood in the count line plotting on how he would get his month supply of canteen since he had no-one sending him money regular like the other inmates. After the officer made his rounds disappearing out of sight nigga was lined up like at the dog betting track throwing packs of noodles, cigarettes and cigars on the floor in the human circle of thugs. One big hefty inmate went as far as to place a bet he made his way through the crowd with a black and white television set cradled in his arms something he knew the CO's

151

would surely snatch during a cell search that ran rapid in the prison system like surprise quizzes in a school setting. PeeWee sat his eight packs in the circle of inmates that circled Pee Wee as he played his role well. He laid out three cards in a row waiting for his victims to place more on the bet pushing up the odds of winning. He waited patiently hoping the red card was not be picked. For he would loose out on eight packs of noodles he didn't possess. As we all know in prison coffee and cigarettes are like crisp one hundred dollar bills. Pee Wee begin to sweat as the big hefty inmate unleashed the cards. He picked up one of the cards calling it out to be a winner before hand. He flipped it over displaying a smile as if he had hit the ten million dollar lottery at the corner 7-11 store.

"These are the red cards like you said they will set me ahead." The hefty inmate said as he took his big hand covering them like tinker toys. Pee Wee stood firm with big round eyes scoping hard hoping this big hefty nigga was wrong. The card he picked up and flipped over revealing an ugly black face.

"Damn!" The big inmate said as he backed up from the table not before growling. He gave the next man a chance to win stepping out of harms way.

"That's it ladies and gentlemen the games are over! Get the fuck away from the table!" Pee Wee yelled as he gathered up his dice and cards. No matter where he went in life whether by bus, train or automobiles in front of grocery stores he would run his game of chance on whoever was willing to put up with it. He would tell them "Put up or shut the fuck up!" this being his favorite line Pee Wee a Chris rock looking nigga. He won many look a like contest with the trophies to prove it. While on the streets hustling became consuming trying to create something from nothing in a matter of minutes if a nigga wanted to eat all the above was necessary.

Pee Wee considered himself a street smart hustler by trade the white man would had loved to get there hands on him this ran continually in his mind. Soon as the day started rain, sleet, snow or sunshiny sky' s. he would go down to the local corner in his home town state of Ohio and stand there waiting for unsuspected victims to cross his path selling game was the only thing Pee Wee could manufacturer and he figured he would never get caught.

He been through his share of ups and down in life just like any man or woman. Born and raised in the ghetto this was like a part time job to him making people feel lucky like lady luck. Living in a roach infested tenement from birth to adulthood made Pee Wee angry and he wanted to strike out. Unable to move to a higher calling was at the top of his dream list. Living without hot water with a pregnant woman he shared his bed with weighted on his mind constantly.

"I'll be back!" Pee Wee yelled after winning five dollars from one of his many unsuspecting victim as he raised the Monte table up lugging it to the next corner.

"Where's my money, nigga." One of his old customers asks as he seen Pee Wee packing from corner to corner using geography as a scape goat He paid one of the many hookers that stood around to act as if she had won so he could draw customers. As she walked up she claimed to know where the red card was located on the table. It was flipped over she won twenty dollars that would be returned to Pee Wee as soon as the con was over. This made people who walked up and down the street want to participate in the activities taking place. Four over dressed thug walked up on Pee Wee's table throwing platinum chains down to place a bet the chain was so heavy it shook the table sending cards scattering. Pee Wee's tongue hung out the side of his mouth wondering how would he cover this bet because there was no way he would let these four motherfucker's walk away with this big thick chain that would pay next months rent. He knew he had to find a way if it meant running.

"Don't know body play this shit no more, man! Three card Monte been played out nigga!" One of the thugs said with an angry voice and look on his face.

"Red will put you ahead while the black will set you back!" Pee Wee said as he shuffled the cards around trying to hypnotize the thugs and surrounding audience with his hands. The hand was quicker than the eyes if Pee Wee told the story.

"The red cards right there, motherfucker!" The thugs friends yelled like big kids in a candy store they bounced around knowing he better had have the money to cover the bet they had just place.

The card was flipped over and eyes started to roam.

"I hope you got a gun or a knot in your pocket to cover this bet! Because the chain cost me one g." The thug reached for the cards as Pee Wee's little hand beat him to the punch.

"You said the red will set me ahead here's the red card right here, nigga!" he pushed Pee Wee down on the ground as the other thugs surrounded him like an ugly big black shadow ready to take his soul if that what it came down too. They waited until the card was flipped.

"Bam!" The Biggest thug said as the card was turned over and the black card revealed its ugly face once again.

Pee Wee bounced back on his feet. To see the Christmas miracle taking place on his corner.

"Damn!" The thug said as his friend fell out laughing because he had lost his platinum chain he paid a g for to a little nigga like Pee Wee. Pee Wee felt threatened. He picked up the cards shoving them back in his deck that's when the thug who lost his thousand dollar chain and his buddies surrounded him.

Where's the chain, nigga?" the biggest one asks. He stood at least three hundred pounds to Pee Wee's hundred and ten.

"I won the chain fair and square, nigga, there's no way I'm given it back!" Pee Wee said no matter how short and slim his body frame was he was willing to put up a fight. Winning wasn't an everyday affair with bills due and a woman who claimed the baby in her belly was his. He was ready to go gangsta on these three nigga's. Just as he thought he had gained an inkling of courage to fight. The biggest thug took off his belt and begins to swing it hitting Pee Wee across his back like a runaway slave. He fell backwards. The thug that lost his chain picked up a metal garbage can that sat nearby and held it over his head. Then boom!

The medal trash pale hit Pee Wee upside the head creating feeling of pain and blood ran everywhere. There was no doubt in Pee Wee's mind these men were out to kill. Blood flowed down his mouth creating a red stream on the sidewalks his ears begun to ring.

"Now, whose gonna put up or shut up!" The thugs said as he searched each and every one of Pee Wee's pockets looking for the chain.

"Where is it?" he asks as he continued to search.

Pee Wee moaned from his injuries, cuts and bruises.

"Where is it, nigga?" the friend of the thug asks.

"I can see we're going to have to kill this motherfucker!" one of them said.

The whole conversation the thugs had over Pee Wee's body as he laid stretched out on the ground as they stood there the thugs never seen it coming.

The streets were clear. All activity that went on during the day had come to a shrieking halt.

Pee Wee knew he was a nice guy at heart but this took the cake. He lifted up the pants leg of his Levi jeans around his shin he carried a small .32 caliber. The thugs stood over him trying to figure out should they kill him or let him go. The con's out weighed the pro's and the killing was about to take place once they killed him they planned on putting his corpse in a car and set it on fire after they cut off his hands and head. They wanted to kill him gangsta style leaving the neighborhood with something to talk about he thought he would shit his pants once Pee Wee heard this.

"Let him go. There is no way I'm letting this con artist ass mother fucker go!" Just as the a big hand came Pee Wee's way he begin to pop caps shooting all three gangsta killing each one-Pee Wee crawled as fast as he could away from the murder scene leaving bloody bodies in his path. Like they say when you kill one man it's not hard to kill another the first one was hard but the rest would be a piece of cake.

This was the day Pee Wee graduated to another level in criminology. He left Cleveland Ohio headed to a bigger and better scene. His pregnant girl friend left him instead of showing support after he told her about the three men he killed trying to defend himself. Pee Wee gathered up the little bit of money he had and bought himself a one way ticket to another dimension that being Las Vegas where he was told dreams come true. He rode the greyhound bus for a total of twenty four hours before it pulled into the depot. Once he stepped off he took a deep breath. He loved the fact that his girl walked out and not visa versa even if she was pregnant with his child after all she never been through nothing in her lifelike Pee Wee he been through Dante's inferno and back. He shook his head and put the past behind him once and for all. Pee Wee walked into the Mirage one of the most prestigious casino in the West he looked around as if he had just stepped on a cloud in heaven. The smell was wonderful as well all the bright lights he peeped through an adjoining door that was attached to the hotel and there sat a line of slot machines and people laughing and bells ringing and change falling creating happy face and smiles.

"I'm home!" Pee Wee said with excitement in his voice "once and for all." He didn't have enough money to purchase a room if push came to shove he would become one of the many homeless that cluttered the streets in this paradise. Pee Wee gained his confidence as he walked through the adjoining door into a gamblers paradise. He walked pass all the bight lights and ringing bells all the way to the back of the casino where there were steps that led up to a long drawn out stairwell? He walked slowly until he reached the top to discover there were many tables lined up side by side as people dressed in their best attire surrounded each one of the semi circle .he could see they all were high rollers spending big money playing for high stakes a sign that read "high rollers" hit Pee Wee's eyes almost immediately. He felt out of place but all the while knowing that this had to be his lucky night or he wouldn't be there. He needed luck like never before. He bust out his rolled up sock he kept his three hundred dollars in and bought three black hundred dollar chips hoping lady luck would smile on him like he had smiled on so many others in the past except the three big nigga's that tried to kill him for the chain he won fair and square, as he walked up to the blackjack table he blew all three chips before taking a seat at this semi circle table across from the dealer. There were seven players in all the game was already in effect so he waited until he was given a cue to place his bet.

Pee Wee laid one of the black chips in the betting circle his primary goal was to win just like each one of the players he could feel it in his bones like a junkie wanting a fix. He knew a majority of people came to the casinos for entertainment purposes like to see a show or walk along the strip shopping or just to see the sights but this night Pee Wee planned on being the center of attention if he could help it one way or another. As he sat there at the black jack table the strip transformed into an adult's paradise light came on displaying a whole array of colors up and down each block people filled the sidewalks all the casinos were in full swing. Pee Wee clocked the dealer's moves as he shuffled the cards from a shoe that sat nearby. He knew the object of this game "a piece of cake." he said to himself as the shoe ejected cards into the dealer's hands. He dealt each player two cards face down.

Pee Wee watched on as the cards and the dealers hands moved like magic just like his did when he dealt cards playing three cards Monte this fascinated him. He knew the hands were quicker than the eyes and planned on beating all odds. The dealer took his cards one face up and one face down. He asked each player sitting at the table to make a decision. Pee Wee looked to the left of him and watched as each player at the table placed their bets. Pee Wee based his decision on the dealers face up card and the two cards he was dealt he could feel he had a winner right there in the palm of his hands.

He made hand signals to let the dealer knew he had reached a decision. He knew he wasn't allowed to touch the cards but wanted to if only he could have bent one up like he did when playing on the streets to peep the hole card. Other players revealed their losses and walked away from the table as he stood there praying his cards were flipped last revealing twenty one.

"A natural." The dealer announced hyping up the total amount of chips Pee wee had won. By the end of the night Pee Wee had the bank and two beautiful show girls by his side waiting for their cut they were willing to go as far as he wanted them too after all he was a winner and a high roller Pee Wee stepped away from the table a ten thousand dollars richer. The night had just begun he bought everyone in the high rollers court a round of drinks and celebrated all night long taking in shows at MGM by the time the night ended Pee Wee was a married man taking vows at the Flamingo wedding chapel to a show girl named Michele his infatuation drove him into a web of seduction, sexual intrigue with bright lights big city. He was in a town that felt like home but had it dangers just like Ohio's ghettos. His new wife he barely knew alerted Pee Wee of an insider's game on the other side of town where he was not familiar she told him the stakes where much higher and she could get him in without a problem this sparked intrigue in his heart.

"Where exactly is this game you're talking about?" Pee Wee asks as him and his new bride laid in his big water bed in the Mirage's high roller suite butter ball naked getting familiar with each other passions in all kinds of positions.

"I think he's having it on the North side tonight they move around a lot. I'll call and find out. Would you like to go? I can arrange everything." Michele said as she covered her big silicon implants with the tiger print comforter. She picked up her cell phone and walked into the bathroom switching as Pee Wee looked on happy that he made the choice to take a chance and come to Vegas because his dreams were coming true just like he felt in his bones.

"It set honey as soon as the sun goes down and all the action takes place that when the game will start. As you can see the action starts in Vegas after dark." Michele said as she stuck her head out the bathroom door before taking a shower.

"Are your friend's big time?" Pee Wee asked. He waited for an answer after all that's what he wanted to meet the top of the line nigga's that ran shit on the North side.

The night quickly came with all the fringe benefits Las Vegas was so famous for. The fine woman, fancy cars sped by Pee Wee and his bride as they flagged down a cab, Pee Wee's wife wore the most revealing outfit that hung in her closet showing all her flesh and then some. The cab sped down the street pass all the tourist flooding the streets on vacation with money to burn. Pee Wee was hypnotized by all the action going on in the streets as well as the casino's the cab drove down I-95 on the strip to an unknown location. He had five thousand in his pocket and a brand new outfit on feeling richer than words grandeur.

"This must be the ghetto part of town." Pee Wee asks as the cab sped passed crack heads and creeps and characters downtown doing their thing that made them feel complete Pee Wee never knocked no ones game.

"This is what we call hell." His wife said as she giggled knowing Pee Wee was not familiar with his surroundings. The cab finally slowed down erecting the two passengers onto the side walk in front of a dark deserted location North side the worst side of Vegas where crime dwelled the bright Lights had faded, the trees there were none the elegant hotels were replaced with abandoned buildings as far as entertainment went there were winos and junkies holding up walls with their lifeless bodies.

"I sure hope this game is worth all of this." Pee Wee stressed.

"I guarantee you it is." His sexy wife said on the way into this abandoned building. Once inside soon as the door closed behind him he was hit over the head as his wife stepped to the side.

"This the nigga you talking about!" A big tall slim character asks Michele as Pee Wee looked up he was hit over the head again with the but of the gun while being commanded to look at the floor once he handed over the five thousand dollars.

160

"Give it to Michele!" the thin tall man said as he shoved into a bag. Pee Wee was tied up and stripped down to his boxers.

"Do your thing Jimmy!" the thin man said as another man bigger and badder stepped up to the plate.

He had a big red gas can in one hand and an eighteen inch machete in the other he opened its top and poured gas all over Peewee's head he swung the machete chopping off both his hands Pee Wee glanced out the side of his eye as he screamed to a high pitch scream he noticed the one who chopped off his hands he seen him in Ohio that he thought he shot and left on the sidewalk for dead.

"Yeah, nigga I know you didn't think I couldn't come to Vegas too especially after you killed my brothers and left me for dead!"

"I don't know what you're talking about. If its money you want take it all! Just let me go you don't have to do all this, man!" Peewee yelled as he laid on the cold floor with no hands in a pair of boxers. His wife stood in the corner down with the whole operation from the start paid to lead Pee Wee to his final destination like a unicorn.

"I saw you as soon as you stepped into the casino, mother fucker!"

"I don't deserve this, man why are you doing this to me?"

The thin character lit a match before he threw it on Peewee's back grabbing the money and Michele by the hand putting a chain on the door so no one including the police and fire department would have a hard time getting into the place to put Peewee's fire out the fire that brought him to Vegas in the first place.

Chapter 9

World of Snakes

In this world where snake rule and bribery is king, Conspiracy vaporized the air we breathe and corruption filled the inner city streets of each and every ghetto all across the United States of America. The day's are face like soldier's using guerrilla warfare tactic in order to survive with firearms packing in a paranoid state of mind on the twenty four seven grind. G's animal instincts became a way of life for him and his brother Cut. G being a target before he was even conceived fresh out the womb and a first born son trained and turned out as a drug dealer before grade school was completed. To make ends meet he sold crack, ecstasy and a variety of other drugs to help his crack addicted mother who loved drugs as a replacement for what she had been stripped of all of her life this covered up excruciating pain from abuse mentally, physically, publicly and sexually all of her life. . G's military mind would take him as far as he wanted to go which is straight to the top.

"I can't take living like this anymore, man." G said to his brother before taking to the block to sling just like every other young black male he knew and grew up within his neighborhood became like a jungle, like living in the bush.

"I'm with you man? Let's just go make some crème. What's up with you and Harris?"

"Fuck, Harris that motherfucker tried to steal some fresh beat I just composed. If it weren't for me he wouldn't even know how to spin!" G said as he stood up stepping on the roach's that inhabited a rug in his mother's living room on the way out the door.

G being a conventional thinker with "the gift" what most of us call "the gift of gab" he possessed it words flowed out of his mouth like hot butter leaving those around him hypnotized. He had no idea what his purpose was in this world but he sure wasn't going down with his boots off. There would be hell to pay if his path was crossed. Music was something all the young gangta's in his neighborhood was into spinning record, rapping or just hanging out at the studio made the day complete hoping to be discovered.

"I heard you're a sort after nigga. So why are you acting hostile today? You know your beat and rhymes are hot, man" His younger brother stood side by side with his older sibling on the corner of Compton's most dangerous neighbor hood of 5th and central. There was no fear of a cop car rollin by since the cops had undercover gave up on this part of town from all the untamable crime going on in the streets there was a code they dared to cross. Drug dealing was the only job these two young men had ever known in their sixteen and seventeen year old lives.

"Who told you man? I was going to wait until I had everything on paper before I sprung the news on y'all." G said to Cut excited inside but not showing it. His brother hugged him hoping something would break in their lives so they could move up and out of Compton to a more sophisticated place and help their mother get help for her drug problem that had taken over her life like a gangrene. Poverty was something these two were use to after waking up to it and lay down in it every night. Material needs and the necessities of daily life, food was a rarity in this household since all money was taken straight to the dope man by their mother on the first of the month and the drug hustle guided them all in vicious circles . Their wouldn't be shelter if public housing wasn't a part of the conspiracy to make their mother and future sista's depended on the system for a means to an end getting comfortable in potential danger zones stuck without an outlet.

He had no idea his preconceived notions about life would be challenged by one of his own friend and future hater .excessive caution was not there. He stood there on the blood soaked corner where many drive by's had taken place. Flower dried up in front of a lamp post reminded him of one of the soldier that fell his life snuffed out by a bullet meant for somebody else.

"This one is for my homie!" G said as he lit up a blunt and took a pull blowing its smoke in the direction of the memorial. Compton had turned out many famous rappers and G just hoped his time would come once and for all. He co-created songs ever since he was a young boy watching some of his role model on the silver screen and on television trying hard to coax the crowds that watched them to their way of thinking. He popped out of it as a car pulled up beside him rolling down its window.

"Hey, man, J wants you to come to the studio. He has somebody he wants you to meet." The messenger said.

"For what man? I have to make some cheese today. This is much important." G said as he stepped back from the car with his hands tucked in his droopy jeans pockets wearing his black tee.

"I don't think that is more important than meeting one of the hottest nigga's on the circuit man this might be your big break!"

"Yeah, I guess your right. I'll be there."

G ran back to the house to get some of the material he been working on. hoping who ever this friend at the studio was would be able to hook him up into the world of production, promotion and distribution where he wanted to be so his work could blow up and he'd be able to live large like some of the rapper's he help blow up by spending his hard earn money on their records. Tagged and labeled in school when ever he went made G want to prove to the world he could be somebody. He remembered through flash backs when his teacher use to tell him he would never amount to nothing because of his low grades on test papers that she practically slung in his face. G had a message he wanted to deliver and if music was the only way he could do it then so be it.

He would address some of the horror's he witnessed on the streets pushing issues through the creative melody of music and the gift. He arrived at the studio with his brother Cut by his side these two rolled like Siamese twins where ever G went Cut wasn't far behind. The building they stepped in had gang graffiti all over it representing Watts, Compton, Pico- Union, Pacoima and East L.A. where just some of the controllers in the hood dwelled. His jaws dropped when he entered the studio and seen the man who could make his life complete and help him use his gift to do it.

The West coast Compton California aka "The hub city". The home of macks, pimps and outlaws, gangs along with the fallen angels with serious criminal positions and shot callers with the bullet scares to prove it. They all came from the same social setting as G trapped trying to claw their way out of Dante's inferno along with half the human race. Compton's a town where seeing a brother bleed was like watching cars pass by on a Sunday afternoon "normal". G knew this was it for him. He'd have to impress this star maker no matter how many haters sat there in his present hoping his shit would fail. He walked in making his peace before he walked over to the insulation booth opening the door to enter. He would now be able to deliver his message. Nobody saw the same shit he seen in his life. He wanted to tell his story the way he seen fit before it drove him crazy in the head like society want it to. There was no other

165

way no matter how many nigga caught an attitude and wanted to stab him in the back after he defaced them for their dirty deeds. The big round microphone was directed in his face as he stood there contemplating what to relay first he had so much shit in his head. The room became silent as the thugs with titles and positions watched him as he begin to speak the words that flowed out of his mouth like hot melted butter penetrated his being. This made everybody in the room have flash backs of all the shit they been through before they blew up but their ego's wouldn't let them reach back and pull the next brotha man up to the same plateau they sat upon like kings.

Each word G spoke brought up issues of poverty. Death and how men ages 10-29 were dying everyday on the regular like soldiers on the battle fields and nobody acted like they gave a fuck to the battle marks and scares from the constant gorilla warfare that went on everywhere. He rapped about the hustling he did staying on the grin while looking over his shoulders and how he needed eyes in the back of his head to see all the devils that lurked all around him like snakes. Living in a state of paranoia was something G was use to. He couldn't afford to be shot down in the streets by one of his own kind like so many others. He knew weapons were easy to come by especially in the hood where he lived and he always wondered why. This just flowed out of his mouth creating a future platinum prospect. Little did Cut or G know that while he was making his dream a reality his mother was at home overdosing on pills and liquor she felt helpless and rundown the streets had taken there toll on her life giving up was the only thing she knew to do. Not knowing that the seed she gave to birth too would be her redemption. As the music came to a conclusion and the heat in the room had disbursed G stepped out the both.

"Damn man you're hot!" J said as he stuck his thumb up letting him know he had captured the right

166

sound and technique for the message he was trying to deliver.

"Sign him!" J's friend the star maker said. He stood up with his big frame wearing dark glasses covering his eyes making them impossible to see. He was big with much muscle that being the back that protected him like body guards. Everywhere he went his rockwella was with him wearing diamond dog collars eating raw steak like a trained Killa.

"I'm in?" G asks as he stepped out the insulation booth with stars in his eyes ready to sign the contract on the dotted line as the piece of paper was drew up and presented. A celebration was in order and Crystal in champagne flute passed around the room along with mega hydro blunts lit for a brand new star had been discovered.

G's brother Cut shook his hand.

"I knew it man. I told you your hot!" Cut said smiling and still in shock he couldn't believe it was all that rang in his mind.

"Where exactly did you get these stories you're telling man?" J asks "That shit almost had me in tears!" he smiled so hard displaying his gold fronts.

G laughed. "This is my life motherfucker and half of the nigga's in this room been through some of the same shit! But act as if their afraid to admit it!" G said as he closed his book of rhymes.

"I want you in L.A tomorrow. I will have everything we need to talk about as far the contract goes. And welcome abroad man!" The star maker James said.

"Thanks man!" G said. Still in shock, slightly shaking inside from his all of a sudden success this was like standing at the cross roads to him ready to take the step that would take him up on the elevator of life. His wish to rise and finally take his place in the sky had come to pass.

"Now what?" G said as he looked lost as James explained the ropes to him letting him know he would guide him through the process.

"I have everything under control all I need you to do is show up downtown tomorrow nine o'clock sharp."

You could tell James was a man who had everything he wanted in life by the way he stood and the way he dressed. The diamonds he sported on one of his hands spelled greed from his thumb to his pinky. G scoped out the fact that James was born with this same gift as he, that being gab. He could move a crowd with all the power he possessed. A natural born sales person who could sale ice to an Eskimo if push came to shove. G shook his hand as James walked over to the studio owner J, and whispers something in his ear, he handed him a white envelope as him and his bodyguards walked out to an entourage of Hummers that were parked curbside the studio door.

"Damn, I can't wait to tell ma you did it, man!" Cut yelled as him and G walked down the block to their spot.

When they arrived their mother's bedroom door was closed, G walked over and opened it with a smile on his face ready to share his news of making it to the big times, he would finally get to help his mother with the addiction that eat at her like a leach. G pushed the door open to find their mother laid out on the floor foaming at the mouth, she was fighting for her life taking her last breath after taking two high strength ecstasy pills. Her eyes rolled back in her head and it appeared that she had thrown up all over the place. G knew for every two people that died from an overdose there were two thousand somewhere looking for that ultimate high. He has been in the streets to long not to know. Cut and G stood over the body petrified and hurt that this would happen on the same day he signed a contract with a prestigious record company that would eventually deliver him and his family from the clutches of their povish lifestyle.

"What the fuck did she take?" Cut yelled hysterical from the discovery.

"Call the ambulance, man!" G yelled back so his brother would gather his thoughts to make the call.

"Damn, mama!" G yelled as he took a blanket off the bed and covered her body not before taking his hands closing her big hazel eyes as they stared at him as if she was still alive.

"What are we gonna do? Man!" Cut yelled to his brother seeing the life as they knew it take quick metamorphoses.

"I don't know just calm down." Just as Cut and G heard the siren coming from a mile away in their direction to take their mother to her finally destination they both took their packages out their pockets dumping the contents in the toilet.

"Man, this shit killed our moms!" G said making a vow to do the right thing in memory of his moms who tried all of her life to provide for him and his baby brother until her addiction took her in a whole nother direction.

This world is designed to sedate the weak knowing eventually some would be taken out via sedation. Using more and more was G's mothers down fall. Living on a fixed income plus suffering from depression. Illusion eventually took place of reality. The invisible line that held her family together began to disintegrate right before her eyes; Drugs became the ultimate escape at a crucial time in her and her son's life. G stood there gazing at the blanket that held the body of the one woman who he loved more than words itself. To see her dead was the last thing he expected when he walked into her bedroom.

G thought about the things his mother use to tell him before she sent him out on the block to become a man at age eight. She explained how she

169

was a courier for an old Jamaican man when she was just a young girl carrying his brother Cut in her belly. She was single and naïve to the true facts to see that her and many other girls her age were doing the same job transporting illegal substances. Unemployed with a baby already low education and poor made thing a whole lot worst then what they appeared to be. Cut took his hat off and bowed his head down saying his last good byes as a tear rolled down his cheek.

"Come here, man." G took his brother in his arms holding him as both of them cried.

"Thugs cry, man." Cut said in a whisper as he wiped his eyes trying to gain a serious composure something that was hard to do at times like these.

There was a knock at the front door.

The police and paramedic came into the house eight deep carrying a stretchers and other medical equipment checking out the scene to see if they had just stepped foot into a crack house that seemed to run rapid in this community. G and Cut took them into the bedroom. The paramedics checked their mother's pulse before writing down the time of death. Once he announced the time and that there was no pulse that made everything official. As the white cop looked at the body of the middle aged black single mother lying there under a blanket he assumed right off that the death was drug related without saying a word. In other words Cut and G's mother was a martyr to low social economic status in America.

G was determined to reach his goal of becoming one of the hottest rap stars in L.A. he believed in himself and the encouragement his family gave him even if his mother was addicted she knew she had two winners in her life that was blessed with potential even if the streets had to teach them their calling.

"Live and learn boys." The white cop said before he walked out the door and closed it behind him.

G knew he had much hard work ahead of him and he was born to do what he had to do in order to take care of his brother who had also been tagged and labeled and put on prescription drugs when he was little boy.

L.A. "The city of Angels" the entertainment capital of the world. G knew it would be up to him to take this town by storm making his mark in this world by gaining recognition along with international fame. The car pulled up to the tall skyscrapers building. G and Cut sat there for a minute to calculate all the stuff that was happening in their lives, things were moving extremely fast. His talents of talking, watching, thinking and working at a very early age would became a part of his style he controlled each ability well. He could be very convincing when trying to sell himself to whom ever along with everything else he controlled the power of influence. He loved an audience and seeked to attract all the right attention in his musical career. The door man held the door of the most notorious music company in L.A. as he walked in feeling powerful the rush was too much to bear.

"Welcome brothers." The black door man said knowing that he never seen these two faces in the building before.

Cut and G took the elevator up to the thirtieth floor where James office sat. He opened the door to find a beautiful secretary seated behind her desk talking on the phone.

"We have an appointment." Cut said for his brother.

"Hold on, girl, just a minute, sir." The secretary said before laying her cell phone on her desk, pressing the intercom system to alert Mr. James Putman his client had arrived for their appointment.

"You can go in." She said before she walked the two youngsters to the door opening it with a grin on her face as she eyeballed G.

171

"G, Cut glad you made it and your on time, now that's what I like as you well know G we have a lot of work ahead of us and I will be handling everything to assure you that everything will run smoothly.

"You will have a recording session tomorrow and from their we'll see what happens, after that it's up to the public." James said as he walked over to the big picture window behind him and looked out while talking.

"I will coach you and guide you all while supervising each and every session you'll be attending."

"First we are going to arrange your material did you bring any music with you?"

Cut and G felt like two small children as Mr. Putnam explained the ropes to G. they could see power was something that Mr. Putnam wasn't a stranger too. He displayed his armor with pride.

"In this business death comes before dishonor." Mr. Putnam said as he looked over his shoulder at Cut and G. as they sat there listening humbly. "That's my philosophy of life anyway." Mr. Putnam said as he moved around his big office. "Be here tomorrow and we will hit the studio and turn out some of your cuts on CD and put them out there." Putnam eyeballed his shrugging off his shoulders with his hands.

G and cut left excited about the adventure they were about to be taken on in the world of music being babies to the game was what worried G. He thought about how many nigga he knew who had been taken on a ride thinking that fame and fortune was what life was all about when in reality it's the least.

His career took off just like he expected it too. His message spread like wild fire all across the country as far as China. Money poured into his pockets like never before. His mother would have been proud if she were still alive to see her son's successes. G laid in his bed thinking about how he needed some one he could depend on solely to keep up with each and every dime of his dividend that calculate just as fast as he made it. He hired a man after word of mouth that he was told was a rich man's dream hiring him on the spot G felt relieved.

G's tour took him half way across the world leaving everything in the hands of the rich man's dream when it came to money. When he returned he was called by an agent to alert him of his finds.

"Hello?" The agent said into the receiver.

""Whose this?" G asks.

"This is agent Banks, Mr. Jones. I'm calling to alert you that your funds have been depleted."

G stood up he didn't have any idea what this agent was talking about.

"In other word Mister Jones you're broke." The agent relayed.

"I have an accountant he handles all my money. So I think you have me mixed up with somebody else!" G yelled into the receiver he knew he worked to hard to get to this point in his career.

"No, your accountant is the one who is ripping you off, Mister Jones. He's been defrauding you ever since you hired him. As a matter of fact he just purchased a plane and brand new mansion in Paris all with your money."

G didn't want to hear no more. He called Cut and alerted him of the phone call he had just received.

"What the fuck do you mean your accountant is ripping you off?" Cut yelled talked on his phone he did a sudden u-turn in the middle of the streets headed for his brother's house.

"Where is that mother fucker?" Cut asks as he enters his brother mansion.

"I haven't spoken with him just yet I was figuring we could ride over to his place how about it

173

are you down?" G asks Cut as they rolled out like soldier looking for a battle.

G stood at the door of his accountant's house banging waiting to get in. while Cut walked around the exclusive luxury property looking for a way in. the person he thought would rip him off this being Mr. Pitman was not the criminal in this case but the one least suspected soul.

"Open the door, man!" G yelled as Cut opened the door from the inside of the house.

"How did you get in?" G asks as he stepped over the threshold to enter his accountant's house. There was doubt he lived the lifestyles of the rich and famous there was pool, exercise facility, library, grand staircase, theater, and a boat house just to name a few of these features that showed he spent the people he ripped off money well.

"I opened the side door this mother fucker is Hugh. Exactly how much do you pay him anyway?" Cut said as he stood there scratching his head ready to fight if his brother needed him too bust up something he was down by law and ready.

G and Cut walked through the luxury home built in the side of a Hollywood hill looking for any and everything they could find to prove to themselves that what the agent said was not true. The way G's accountant lived you could see he accumulated more money and assets then the stars he worked for. G was unaware of the lavish lifestyle his hand picked money grubber lived. He found paper work and travel brochures of foreign trips his accountant been on. Not to mention his accountant sent his children to all the best schools from Switzerland to Paris. He drove an expensive plush Bentley and other top of the line automobiles he purchased at the expense of G and others like him. G thought back to the powerful presentation this man made using the same gift as he that being gab before he was coaxed into letting this man keep count of his millions and G fell for it.

He stood there mad at the world for letting him down the dream he had achieved was snatched back just as fast as it was issued into his life. He realized at this point he had been stabbed in the back and immediately became paranoid. His search in life for justice for the unjustified lead him to bankruptcy and a whole line of problems to follow all brought about by not keeping his eyes on the person he hired to watch his money. Leaving his destiny in the hands of trained professionals with bachelor's degrees.

Chapter 10

Shot House

The shot house is a place where deals are made and philosophies exchanged. The hour was two a.m. in the morning as the customers filled Grady's shot house this was considered to be the happening place after hours. If you didn't attract a man at the club you could meet one at Grady's this was a proven fact. If you wanted to get laid you could get laid at Grady's along with every other vice under the sun. This was all a part of the concept. The house stayed packed with crap games going on in one room while the card games went on in another. The money was stacked on the table and expensive cars parked outside which was a sure clue that playa's was inside the house gambling. Grady stood guard over the three card tables like a drill sergeant so he could get his cut from the winners if somebody just so happened to win. Susie poured the drink. The smell of alcohol and smoke filled the air along with laughter and gossip. There was a loud knock on the door but the party still went on.

"Come on in!" Grady yelled as he stood there ready to open it for his guest. This was the night all drinks were half off thus generating customers. He opened the door doing his bouncer's job only to be knocked down on the floor disrespected in his own place of business.

Four armed men wearing mask made there way pass the house man into the living room that was packed with hookers and the dates and other paying customer's and the midnight prowler looking for pussy on the sly after the clubs closed.

"This is a hold up ladies and gentlemen!" the four robbers burst through the door pimping locking it behind them for security purposes. They planned this robbery for a long time coming even casing out the joint from time to time. Guns were displayed and pointed in the house man face along with his guest who inhabited the living room area. The people in the gambling room had no idea a robbery was in progress.

"Who are you? And what do you want?" Grady asks as he remained on the floor shocked that a robbery was in session. Perlbition didn't have nothing on Grady's shot house. He catered to the best of them sometimes even famous people stop by for a shot of liquor creating a buzz in the community thus generating capital and more customers the place became sort of a landmark. Each one of the mask men armed with glocks were ready to use them if their orders weren't followed.

"Everybody in this motherfucker house strip!" one of the thugs yelled as they all looked serious as heart attacks with a black and white bandanna's tied around their mouth and over their face with the military tactical gear outfits. Each female in the house screamed they wasn't about to expose their goodies to every man in the place. The back door opened where the gambling took place the bouncer that was supposed to protect the house man from event like this one was in the back room gambling he had no idea what was taking place until he stepped foot out the back room into the living room.

"Look at what we have here!" One of the robber yelled out as he walked towards the back room and seen the gambling table surrounded with playa's from the hood wearing big hats with some of the flies honey in Philadelphia area on their arms sitting there at the table profiling trying to get their gamble on.

"Shit is looking up in here! Nigga's we hit the fucking jackpot. These mother got at least ten g's on the table. The robber danced around the table as he took the bag he held racking all the money chips and all off the table into the bag all while holding his gun in the face of the bouncer.

Grady looked over at the robber's and then the bouncer. He tried to make eye contact and then make a slick move but before he could pull himself up off the floor the handle of the glock hit him across the head creating a knot while knocking him out cold.

"If anybody, I mean anybody tries to make a fucked up move like that one I'll put a bullet hole in this motherfucker's head! Take all your mother fucking jewelry off and put it in the motherfucking bag! Plus all underwear should be off by now after you finish that y'all bitches line up against the wall!" The robber took his gun and swayed it over the crowds head. The line was forming against the wall while his partner searched each and every person's pockets, taking all valuable sticking them into the bags along with all the other valuables before looking for the safe. That was the whole point of this robbery to get to Grady's safe. Word on the street this old man held onto millions in shoe boxes and in a safe that was hidden in the wall in his house.

Grady's spot was the hottest spot in town this is where all the fly thugs came for drinks after hours after the clubs closed their doors, there just so happen to be a couple of defenseless thugs in the house on the night of this robbery wearing expensive platinum chains and watches with filled up money clips in their pockets. "That's right playa's take everything off including your underwear!" the robber said as he stood there watching and laughing because of the intimidating power he possessed, at this moment in time. He knew he could get nigga to lick a another nigga balls if that's what he wanted after all he was the one holding the fucking gun and if he said jump a nigga better had ask how high or get shot.

"Now, house man you bring your slick ass on over here and show Johnny where the safe is locate and when you locate it, open it!" the robber yelled in Grady's ears as he grabbed him by the arm and pulled him towards the kitchen where a variety of liquors sat. The robber took hold of a shot glass and poured himself a shot of patron drinking it on the spot. Then quickly poured himself another as a chaser. Grady stood there defenseless to the powers that be; he had a flash back as if his life would be snuffed out right in front of his eyes with the handle of glock 27 that almost knock the life out of his seventy year old body. He thought back when it all began for him and how he use to transport hooch over the state line for many, many years before he could set up shop. Then here comes a bunch of young thugs to rob him of his whole life's savings. He spent the money just as fast turning laundered money into tangible goods such as real estate and buying car when ever the spirit hit him for years he had so much material goods he couldn't keep up with it all age had taken it's toll. His mental state was not tight his ego had inflated not knowing how the streets had changed since Perlbition. He trusted each and every stranger he opened his shot house doors too. Knowing the neighborhood was getting bad but he never figured it would turn as tragic as this. Grady reached under the cabinet to the hidden compartment under the kitchen sink and pulled out a safe like the armed men demanded.

All eyes that were lined up against the wall turned their nude bodies in surprise to see if the urban legend was true about Grady having a safe loaded with money, the women stood there against the wall holding their hands over their private not wanting to expose too much too soon.

Philadelphia was where Grady decided to open his first shot house back then the old heads called it a speakeasy, all the incoming money started to stack up from the liquor sale scaring the shit out of Grady. He handed the safe over with a tear rolling down his cheek. The robber snatched it.

"What took you so long grandpa? If you would have did this earlier all this wouldn't have never happened!" the robber said as he pushed the old man on the floor.

"I want to have a little fun before I leave." One of the robbers told the other ones.

"What nigga! Let's get the fuck out of here after he opens the safe."

Grady crawled over to the safe taking hold of the spin wheel in his hand he looked over at the four masked men as he spinned out the combination, it opened so much money was stuffed in it money fell out all over the floor not to mention stocks and bonds and silver bars.

"Wow, who would have ever known all this was locked up in such a shack!" One of the gangsta said. A felony was nothing to these men they been intimidating people ever since they could walk, stealing money from the weak and giving it to themselves the strong.

"Since you took so long to give us the safe I'm killing everybody in here, everybody get on your knees." The gangsta robber cocked his glock the woman and men shed tears in fear of dying from the toughest nigga's in the room cries rung out in the air but unheard in the street.

"Hey, man I gave you what you wanted. Just go on now why kill everybody in the room?" Grady asks trying to spare innocent lives from his mistake of not putting all his

Money in the bank like all the other hustler's in the community. There was a variety of businesses he could have specialized in. In his seventy years from smuggling, loan sharking, book making, prostitution. He knew a lot of young ladies strung out that would sell their bodies just because he asked them too for a couple drink and little conversation. The porn business paid good even if the pimp is a senior citizen, pussy would sell there was no doubt about it. He could have even ran a crew to high jack cargo trucks if he chooses too. But he choose to open a shot house instead. Grady felt this was his calling in life to satisfy the hungry souls of the lonely for a price per shot. His services were much needed in the community when a man or woman needed an ear to listen to their complaints or just a shoulder to lean on with a drink to wash away the blues. Grady handed the safe to the arm robber's before two of them grabbed him by the hand and took him in the empty gambling room and putting him through a variety of changes before they both shot him, each intended victim cringed from the shots being heard in the next room. The robber's came out the room holding his smoking glock up in the air with out conscious regrets as he went for the ladies. He took one of Grady's long time customers and friend Sadie in the same room. Once he closed the door she screamed each and every victim could only image what he was doing to her in the back room. When the door open he stepped out zipping his pants as his home boys each took turns with her before shooting her in the head.

"Wait a minute man! Wait a minute" One of the naked thugs said as he held his hands up as if he was being searched by the police.

"Wait for what, man?" The robber asks as he went for him.

"You have no say so in this matter. We are not leaving no witnesses behind this deal is locked stocked and barrel." He took the tough guy into the same room as an array of bullet shot him in the chest. Blood seeped from under the door sending the victims into a panic and the ladies that remained into a state of shock.

The money Grady left behind was more than enough but the robbers insisted on taking souls along with this hold up. The name of their game was if no witnesses are left alive, no one can talk or point them out to the authorities if they are eliminated on the spot. The money was split three ways in Grady's kitchen as the robbers watched the last of the victims standing there against the wall crying, praying, confessing, and a variety of other penances were going on.

"Can a man at least have a last drink before he get shot?" A man asks as he stood there with his hands barricaded over his penis.

"I don't see any harm in that." The youngest robber said as he took hold of a bottle of liquor and poured the man a drink.

The man came up for air after the quick gulp down of the liquor, as the other's watched on. They all wanted a drink to wash down their fears of being shot as soon as the feeling hit one of the robbers.

"Can I have a drink?" One of the hookers that remained against the wall asks. The young thug assisted her.

As he turned his back smiling and laughing with his accomplices in crime. The bouncer grabbed the thug's gun.

"See man you done went and fucked up now!"

"Fuck that!" The bouncer said as he pointed the gun directly at the robber's head. He exposed his privates not caring who seen them at this point.

"Y'all told me when you planned on hitting this joint up that I would get half that money for setting the whole thing up!" the bouncer was past hysterical.

"Oh...Lord!" The hooker cried out.

"No you didn't set Grady up!" She yelled out.

"Shut up, bitch!" The bouncer yelled shifting the gun in the hooker's direction.

"He was on his way out anyway and plus he wasn't paying me enough, that mother fucker had a safe filled with money but yet he only paid me six dollar's an hour, What motherfucker do you know who can support his family off of six dollars an hour.

"Listen up man you got it just put the gun on the floor!" the robber's pleaded as they backed up from the money strolled across the kitchen table and took their place on the wall where the rest of the victims lined.

"I want all the money not half but all! After all I worked all my life like a slave for it and Grady never once gave me my props!" The bouncer said.

"I don't have nothing to do with that I just know if I owe you man I'll pay you so put the gun on the ground.' The robber yelled trying not to get shot like Grady and the others.

"Get over there and strip like you made me strip mother fucker!" The bouncer yelled as he went for the safe.

"All y'all motherfuckers turn around!" He yelled.

The robbers took one more look at the bouncer before they stripped and turned around like they were all ordered to do. The bouncer went bazzerk shooting each and every person that remained against the wall of terrors, even his long time friend. He opened the door for, for years became targets to his revengeful plot to run with the blood money he watched Grady collect and stick in a safe. He plotted this robbery for a long time to come hiring the neighborhood thugs to carry it out. He remembered days he ask for a raise only to be ignored by his long time friend and employer. The night of the robbery he was told to go in the back room and gamble so that the robber's could come in and take shit over the feeling of anticipation took the booker over. He wanted Grady dead for his disrespect and disappointments using him as a servant for so many years.

The bouncer was never caught but lives his life looking over his shoulder from the lies. Schemes and deaths he caused not enjoying the fruits of his labours.

Chapter 11

White Slavery

Howard exited his long stretch Cadillac buttoning his long black leather jacket. He was a sure enough playa in the streets of Miami at least he thought he was. He slammed the car door behind him taking some spit slicking back his stringy black Puerto Rican hair. As he walked up to the barn that sat behind an old farm house at the end of a dead end road at the end of one of Miami Florida's secluded areas. Howard knocked using a secret knock in order to be let in. The big wooden door opened as the smell of musk and urine hit Howard in his nose he stepped forth into the door under a horse shoe hanging overhead. This was the night a display of all the new girls who had been caught and held as captives by force by Bob the trafficker. Forced into a world of white slavery turning tricks for little or no profit at all the ladies and young girls were escorted out the back room a section that had been specially built to hold them. Blind folds of the blazing color red covered their swollen eyes along with black fist rings that had been continually inflicted at the hand of violent traffickers.

"Howard." Bob the trafficker yelled as Howard closed the barn door behind him hooking the latch that kept the traffickers and sex slaves safe from the outside world. Howard walked over giving his partner in crime a hand shake and hug mafia style. Howard's confidence was high; he knew for every four or five girls he picked to work for him there was 14,000 being shipped every minute of the day becoming ponds in the world's biggest international trade of commercial

185

sexual exploitation he just so happen to be just one of the many playa in this game.

"I'll be taking two girls tonight, Bob." Howard said as if he was ordering an order of fries from a fast food joint. He walked towards the goods on display checking out their legs, teeth, hair, looks and size before the purchase. This was an important routine that each trafficker took as a number one rule the property had to be in tip top condition in order to get the full asking price.

"Only two Howard?" the trafficker asks knowing Howard was famous for asking for at least a dozen girls at a time like buying eggs at the local seven eleven store.

"That's right, I have enough problems already man. I'm getting too old for this shit. Been thinking about retiring after this run."

"Retiring? There's too much money to be made out there especially in this state to be thinking about retiring now. Howard." Bob said as he lined the girls up along the barn house wall they all appeared to be scared and petrified but was told they would be shot dead in the streets if they ever tried to escape or signal for help when ever a male customer or client came around looking to buy.

"I have two blondes for you right here been holding them hoping you would show up to see me." The trafficker said as he whispered to Howard as if he was telling him a big secret.

"What?" Howard asks.

"These two are not from here either. I placed an ad in the news paper, that's how I lured these two beauties." Bob said as he made what he did for a living look normal instead of inhuman.

"And guess what Howard? One of these beauties is a virgin."

The trafficker laughed knowing virgins where worth money top dollar.

"How do you know that she's a virgin?" Howard asks as he crossed his arms standing there.

"There's a cruise ship coming in and if you need some more woman or girls anytime soon just let me know. You know I'll bring them to you if you can't pick them up. I got my boy's working that ship their apart of the crew on board, he scouts them out then bingo bring them straight to me just like working on an assembly line." Bob said laying the whole kidnap scheme at Howard's feet.

Howard was silent for a minute he begins to contemplate. He had to weigh things out in his mind before making this serious career move he wondered was this risk worth taking.

"Put them in the car." Howard announced as he handed Bob a big yellow envelope filled with fifties and hundreds.

Bob became extremely happy. He motioned his hands for his side kicks in crime to put the two girls in Howard's car both being under age they did their business in a discreet manner. He strung the rest of the prisoners up before taking them back to the back room of the barn where they were all crammed into a little space sitting side by side on the floor waiting for further orders. Howard's chosen profession was that worst then a pimp. He seen mother's who had been bitten by the poverty bug in the streets and desperate to selling their own daughters to traffickers in order to have enough food to fill their stomachs for one night. He saw woman and young girls through out his life who begged him to put them to work in the sex business to make extra money to survive on the streets before become consumed by it. he even went as far as to arrange forced marriages in his younger days Howard remembered luring, deceiving and manipulating using intimidation tactics even blackmail to seduce that's how his bank account grew to unlimited amounts of monetary unit from all around the world with that came respect and lot's of power to top it all off. He arranged marriages where men wanted woman who wouldn't talk back but did their wifely duties by force in a locked down environment where escape was extremely impossible. Howard drove his car to an undisclosed location with his two new buys lying to the side in the back seat. He dared them to make a move. He drove through

The streets of Miami knowing that he wouldn't be stop. This is how much confidence he had in his self. He drove knowing he knew the location to which he was taking them.

"Ah...Ah" the blonde hostages moaned as their hands where painfully pulled behind their back with a thick black cord bound them tightly together. The thick darkness of night rang out

As Howard continued to drive passing by all the freak that inhabited the streets looking for something immoral to get into once the sun went down. The car came to a complete stop in the middle of no where there was no noise or a car in sight nor any car horns being blown there was not a plane, bus or train passing by in this area just the sounds of crickets and other unknown animals filled the empty void called night.

"Ah..." Both girls became extremely loud with their moans making Howard extremely nervous in his own skins. Pulled both girls out of the car escorting them both through a tall grassed area where the grass was so tall it hurt the skin when it hit it. The two girls could hear they weren't alone. Others screamed out from the grass shouting and yelling to be set free like spirits kept bound. The noise became louder with the sounds of moans and sexual moans from men that had paid heavily to be with these abducted captives.

Howard took a piece of card board box that he had lined up through out the large stretch of land. He would collect money from the men from all walks of life that wanted pleasure which Bob provided by capturing all kinds of girls the sneakier the method

188

the more the thrill Howard thought in his twisted mind. All the girls he kidnapped, lured, abducted on the regular basis were all forced to have sex with strange men in other words they were raped by men with no consciousness that took full advantage while these girls hands was bound behind their backs. Howard had a cold heart when it came to woman and it showed money meant more to him then being human.

"Howard, let me go please. I can't take it no-more." A young girl yelled out from the tall grass not knowing that no one cared or even heard her cries for help because Howard owned each square inch of land that each woman and young girl occupied.

"Shut up!" Howard yelled back emotionally cold and uncaring.

The noises became louder and louder driving Howard crazy. He drove off leaving the girls to fin for themselves in the middle of nowhere blind folded and bound laying on cardboard boxes in the tall grass.

He knew the time to close down shop was at its peak. Premonitions begun to take over his mind the feelings that the authorities would be moving in on his businesses ran continually occupying his head. He had to come up with a plan in order to retire in style leaving a bunch of dead young girls on his trail. He wanted to get the most for all the money he spent thus deciding to sell each girl to the sex industry before taking off going back to Puerto Rico. He knew a couple of guys in the industry that he could confide in asking them to take on his girls for a satisfactory price. He dialed rolled up to a shop where sex toys, peep shows and lots of erotic products were being sold. He knocked on the back door waiting to be let inside the establishment.

"Howard." The tall slender man said when he opened the door Howard was always greeted with enthusiastic hellos. He was the man that could get you turned on if sex was what you were looking. The local police department forensic men had nothing on Howard, he was treated like a king every where he went. Many men knew Howard was into illegal trafficking selling young girls and woman against their will.

"Hi man." Howard said as he brushed up against Jeff going in the door. Jeff looked both ways before letting him in hoping the cops was not trailing undercover behind him.

"What brings you to this part of town? I thought Miami seen the last of you. You haven't been by in such a long time." Jeff said locking the door behind him.

"I got a proposition for you. I have two young girls I want to sell to you to put in your shop. You can use them for peep shows or what have you." Howard said trying to sell the product to the highest bidder like a PR making deals.

"Woe… I don't need that kind of business in my store it took me too long to get business off the ground to let two beautiful girls ruin all this. I have the police sniffing around here already. I can image what they'll do to me if I put two under aged girls in my show."

"I'll have to pass on this one this time, Howard." Jeff said as he walked back to his cash register counting his day's earnings.

"Come on do me this one favor this time. I promise you these two will bring in big bucks." Howard expresses trying to make Jeff see the profits margin of the whole deal that the two would generate.

"Suppose I bring them into my world and then one tries to escape how would that look for the business. I'm trying to run a respectable shop here on the strip." Jeff said as he stepped back hoping Howard would just leave.

"Where are these two girls you're talking about anyway?" Jeff asks looking through the window at Howard's car not seeing any kind of movement or any blonde haired woman in the back seat.

"Oh, you know where I keep the product. If you change your mind let me know.' Howard said disappointed that Jeff wouldn't take the two blondes off his hands so he could leave town on the first thing smoking. Howard's walked down the strip a little further where his

Boy Charlie ran the best lap dance house in town. Charlie stood outside his establishment with a big cigar hanging from his mouth. He had a young lady that was made up to look like a full grown woman standing beside him. The cigar fell to the ground when he noticed Howard walking up on him.

"Howard you almost scared the living shit out of me!" The big bellied man grabbed his heart as they both start laughing.

"Come on inside." Charlie put his hand around Howard's shoulder as they both walked inside his neon lit lap dance room where dances were being performed all day and night long the souls of the dancer were all owned and controlled by him.

"What can I do for you? Howard." Charlie asks as they took a seat at the bar as Charlie ordered the bartender to bring him a round of drinks for him and his friend Howard.

"I have a proposition for you, Charlie." Howard said as the bar tender walked over sitting a bottle of whiskey down and two shot glasses.

"What kind of proposition?" Charlie asks knowing he heard proposition on a twenty four hour level the deal would have to burn his ears for his approval.

"I have two girls I'm trying to unload I know your going to love them because their both sure shot winners. They'll bring in money that's why I had you in mind. So what do you say should I go get them?" Howard said as he stood there about to ask for money then he paid for them this was a part of the juggling game that came with moving bodies.

191

"Go get em if you think your product could spruce up the place how could I say no." Charlie said he was open for suggestions when it came to bringing in new ass he knew money was sure to follow.

"I would never let you down Charlie we've known each other for far too long now."

Howard helped himself to a shot of liquor while making proposition once he had Charlie sold on his proposition. He left the neon lap dance bar driving off through the streets of Miami Beach Florida with propositions and negotiations running through his mind like wild water rapids. Howard knew the police would be moving in on him in a matter of time before long he would throw up the innocent's souls he held in front of him as human shields to block the trouble he had headed his way. Howard pulled up to the tall grassed area only to find that some of the girls he had tied and bound had gotten loose and escaped the scene leaving the other girls behind selfishly Howard went bezzerk.

"What the hell is going on? How did they get loose?" Howard said to himself he knew at this point the hour glass had been turned upside down and time as he knew it was getting short. He took the two blonde haired girls sticking them in the car they were too weak to fight back. The car sped off once again headed back to Charlie's lap dance joint.

Once Charlie laid eyes on the product dollar signs flashed in front of his eyes. Howard's spirits shot up Charlie bust out a big envelope handing it to Howard.

"Now let's see if any of these girls can dance." Charlie said as he flopped his over sized behind on the bar stool Howard sat down beside him waiting to see if the two blondes could dance because he hadn't a clue. The music came on and the neon lights changed there colors as the two stood there looking like two lost children like they were.

"What are you waiting for dance? Charlie said. He had a rough touch with his girls letting them know he didn't take no junk not from man, woman, chick or child. He waiting patiently as he sat there looking each one of the blondes from head to toe. Each girl looked at the other waiting for each one to make a move first. One of Charlie's old dancers told each girl to follow her led. She took the floor wearing her expensive see through lingerie as she slowly walked over to Charlie as she let loose right in front of him he took his shot glass smiling from ear to ear she turned around with her ass rubbing all over his big body and he loved it.

"See this right here. This is how you will do when a man comes in my club looking for a lap dance.

Each blonde started to cry knowing they would never see their families again the feelings took them over. Howard knew he was wrong for his part in their plight but money spoke louder than pussy and words or family.

"I can't do it." The virgin said as she held herself wrapping her arms around herself.

Charlie got off his bar stool and walked over slapping her hard on the cheek her head turned.

"Get over there and dance." He said as he waited for her to take the order he just gave her.

"I can't." She said again just as she did the other blonde walked over towards Howard doing what was expected of her. She swayed to the music propping her behind in Howard's lap as the music's sensual melody helped her body move just right. Howard's man hood became extremely hard.

"Your friend seems to know her place in this operation already. I'll expect for you to do the same. And if you don't you will find your self some where else. You see this operation I run here is based on the pleasure principle men pay me to have you make them happy and if you think there is going to be a problem with this let me know now and we will

193

straighten this before Howard leaves. What ever the decision you still will not see your mother and father ever again do you understand this?" Charlie said as if he was the mafia." I'm going to teach you what it takes to be a woman. Take this one to my office." Charlie stresses as he walked back over to the bar and sat down beside Howard as he watched one of his trained pets carry out his biddings. Charlie had spunk and power in his arena of the sex industry men knew where to come if they wanted some underage woman to fulfill their sick fantasies. He learned the game while living in the Bronx he learned from some of the most powerful men in the district. Mafia was the name of this game back in the seventies until an unexpected turn of events landed Charlie in Miami Beach Florida to retire. He took all of his money opening up a line of tittie bars and lap dance joints once he established himself money and men became his best friends. Some of the old heads he ran with from Brooklyn to Queens would pop into town from time to time looking to spend lots of money on girls old enough to be their daughters knowing that their biggest secrets of being child molesters would never get out. They knew no one wouldn't be the wiser including their wives who thought they had their husbands privates on lock down. If they only knew the sick perverted men they were married to.

"I think I better be going I have a plane to catch." Howard said as he turned the last shot of Jack Daniels up to his wet lips. He slammed the shot glass down on the bar and clutched his leather inside pocket to assure himself the envelope that contained a couple of thousand of dollars would not fall out.

"It was nice doing business with you Howard don't be a stranger when you pop in from Puerto Rico. Howard walked to his Cadillac feeling extra confident and tipsy. He would be on the next plane out if things went his way. He opened the trunk of his car when he did a big black briefcase sat there he opened it and stuck the big yellow envelope in there with the rest of the money he had collected from his part in the sex game industry he was set for life. As he closed the truck two mask men stood there one with a bat the other with a gun.

"Give me the briefcase son." The one with the bat announced and the mask man with the gun cocked his weapon ready to shot if his demands weren't met.

"Get the fuck out of here, mother fucker you have got to be crazy if you think I'm giving a couple of punks my mother fucking money I work hard for all of my life. Just as Howard went to open the car door and stuck one foot inside his vehicle the gun went off.

"I told you to give me the briefcase obviously you don't give a fuck about your life." The mask man with the gun said as Howard clutched his side as the thick red blood ran through his fingers and down his black leather coat.

"Shoot that motherfucker again." The bat carrying thief said as he held the bat up to Howard's head before he took a swing like a batter for a major league team. Howard fell to the grown as the bat cracked something.

Pictures flashed in front of Howard's eyes of the faces of each young innocent girl he had ever abducted in his life he could feel that the last two souls he held in front of him was not protecting him like he expected. He knew the hour glass must have been empty for this to be come at him. He thought of all the times his end would come at the hands of the law when the entire time destiny had his end already mapped out from his birth to his death. The mask men took what they wanted but not before pumping Howard full of holes first. He laid in the streets the one place he ran all of his life from his youth to old age. He contributed to that old cliché about blood running in them his blood being freshly donated by the hands of street thugs.

Chapter 12

When Destiny Comes Calling

When I think of destiny I think of fate things will happen only if they are preordained too as it is written done and said. Ronald laid upon his bed thinking of ways to come up with the cash to pay some overdue bills that seemed to have taken over his life. He thought of whom he could go to and borrow the money before his whole world as he knew it came crashing down all around him from lack of money. The thought became totally frightening all at once just thinking about it. He tossed and turned crinkling his sheets on the cot he slept upon not knowing what to do in order to not loose fate. He would have to plot a little bit harder than usual a time limit had been placed on his head like a death sentence execution would be carried out in a couple of days. He wondered why society would pressure him making him contemplate doing crazy things to whom ever in order to give the bill collectors the money they demanded. Ronald came up with a plan this plan would be one of great risk putting innocent workers and people at risk. Ronald planned on robbing a bank but first he would have to become a part of the establishment in order to lay out the floor plan. Ronald got out of bed putting on his clothes he wanted to be there as soon as the bank opened its doors early that morning.
He knew he would have to become an inside man.

Ronald slipped on his double breasted suit.

"Perfect." Ronald said as he stood in front of the mirror to take a look at the outfit that would get him in the door and a job he had optimistic thoughts running through his mind knowing that once inside and gain the trust of a chosen few his life of need and want would finally be over. Ronald passed his interview with flying colors and was granted the job as a security officer at the Detroit National savings and Loans he walked away with a smile on his face knowing he could handle the job and rob this bank all by his self.

Chapter 13

Money is The Root of All Evil

In society today a man would kill his own mother for a hit of dope all for the evil end money could bring if sort after for all the wrong reasons. Money seems to be able to make the smartest man loose his mind and become greedy. And the simplest of men come up with a plan to get lots of the green stuff. Things are totally out of control in the streets in this twenty first century. This story takes you behind the scenes of the most common of hustlers the hustler of the streets Daniel aka Dick at least that's what the woman called him on the streets in the hood since on rainy days he did a lot of sling his. Daniel walked down Nostard Avenue in the heart of Brooklyn knowing he had control of his surroundings. He was the king in the hood where he grew up he knew everybody on the block from the old heads to the youth just getting out there on the block learning how to make money by hustling. Dicks hustling trait was to get all the money he could, any way he could, while he could and no one would be the wiser to his methods not even the cops that he swore he could out smart. He caught the train to Manhattan where all kind of activity flowed like water this was a hustlers paradise from the jobbers, to the jostlers, even the pimps and ho's flowed when it came to getting that dollar bill. He walked up and down the blocks of Manhattan selling merchandise that fell off the back of a truck to whom ever would buy it. Buy low and sale high was the secret that made him into the person he was on the street and he carried a title along with all the hustling he did 'hustle man' was his name in the streets.

"I got what you want and I got what you need." Daniel yelled as he lugged an arm load of hot dresses on his shoulder. He didn't compare himself with other hustler since they all lived by a code.

An officer from the New York City Police department rolled up on him asking him where did he received all the dresses because he didn't have a sells receipt or a license to sell his wears on the streets in their jurisdiction. Daniel took off by foot slinging dresses on the sidewalk as he ran knowing what was lost would be gained once again no hustle was worth going to jail for in his eyes. He turned down an alley way as the cop car pulled up behind him blocking his escape. He drops the remainder of the dresses on the ground ready to surrender to the authorities by throwing his hands up in the air.

"Drop any and all weapons on the ground!' The black cop yelled as he pulls his revolver out and pointed it in Daniels direction as his white partner sat behind the staring wheel shining his spot light in Daniels face using each and every dirty trick in their dirty cop book to manipulate him.

"I don't have no weapons please don't shoot me man!" Daniel yelled as his heart beat fast like the thump of an African drum almost jumping out his chest.

"No weapons. Huh." The white cop yelled as he fired one shot in Daniels direction scaring the hell out of him he wanted Daniels full attention and this gave it to him.

The black cop looked at his partner shaking his head he knew how hot headed he could be when it came to the African American male running from the cops.

"I don't believe this one don't have a weapon. Half the culture packs so there is no way you're going to tell me we are going to let him go, hell no. Go get him." The white cop told the black one. The officer of the law walked over to Daniel with confidence in his stride before he hand cuffed him pushing him into the cop cruiser.

"What the hell am I being arrested for officer?' Daniel asks with a look of suspicion on his face. The car took off without any of his questions being answered. It sped through the streets of Manhattans through hells kitchen headed to an unknown location.

"Where exactly are you guys taking me, the police department is that way." Daniel yelled from the back seat as he positioned his body on the edge of his seat. The two predator cops paid none of the words coming out of his mouth no never mind. His word meant nothing to men like them they ran shit out there on those mean ass streets and no two bid three time loser could make them think any different the rules to the game was all constructed and made by them.

Daniel could feel that something was not right and he feared for his life. The cop continued to drive with hard looks on their faces. The car finally came to a complete and sudden stop in the front of an abandoned building. The building looked as it could have been a department store before gangrene set in.

The big heavy set black cop snatched Daniel by his jacket collar and drug him out of the police cruiser.

"What's going on man all I was doing when you arrested a brother was hustling some dresses all this ain; t necessary." Daniel said as his body hit the hard concrete sidewalk that laid between him and the arresting officer when the cop proceeded to pull him out of the car. His partner sat on the side of his seat with his feet hanging out of the car on his radio. Daniel listens in as he made a distress call. He knew he was about to get shot.

"What are you two planning on doing to me?" Daniel asks knowing something illegal was about to take place. The white cop stepped out of the car knowing back up would be coming in a matter of minutes and all he had to do was say the word he got a gun and bullets would fly.

"What is it y'all want?" Daniel said looking like a scared child in the face.

"I know you just heard me on the radio and as you know back up will be here in a minute. The only way you could walk away from all this right now would be you will have to work for us."

Daniel throat became dry and parched he knew in the back of his mind the police department housed good cops and bad cops and these two where defiantly bad falling off the rottenest of trees they even wore their uniforms looking like two gangster's. He stood straight up listening to what the cop was about to say he hope it wasn't too crucial what ever words spilled out of the cops crooked mouth.

"This will be your new job if you don't follow my rules this could get real ugly." The white cop said as he stood in the front of the black cop like a shadow.

"What is it man, damn a brother can't even step out the house without this kind of bullshit coming in his direction." Daniel said.

The black cop that seemed to be ruled by the white one stepped from in the shadows holding three big hefty bags of weed straight from Panama they all had red markings on the bags the bags where so big Daniel giggled to himself.

"You're going to sell this for me and when you finish I have another job for you." The white cop walked back over to his cruiser and sat back down on the side of the seat and cancelled his distress call.

"Is everything alright Officer Briggs?' the dispatcher asks.

"Everything's ok." Officer Briggs said before he got out of the car closing the door.

"The corner I picked you up on 140th street will be yours to work from." Daniel thought about it he knew he couldn't win for losing. After all this was the police making him an offer he couldn't refuse.

"Do I have a choice in the matter?" Daniel answered.

"Actually no you don't have a choice in this matter especially if you don't want to go to jail and then who knows the penitentiary and me I might get a plague or maybe a promotion for sending you there." The white cop said before him and his partner laughed. The black cop handed Daniel the three huge bags of weed in a black duffle bag before taking his hand cuffs off.

"If you do this right you might get to graduate to a whole nother level." He laughed before pulling off in the cruiser with his partner in crime.

Daniel knew these two meant strict business and he also knew they also would give him enough rope to hang himself in the end if he slipped up. His mind work overtime trying to come up with a scheme to scheme the two crooked cops out of all their weed and the money that would accumulate from the sales of the illegal substance.

"Damn." Daniel said as he grabbed his privates and spun around. He knew the streets wasn't nice to him like they had been in the past shit was all of a sudden getting real stinking and wicked and to top it all off. Daniel had nothing to loose so he decided to give the two cops what they wanted. Daniel called a couple of his boys creating a crew to help him sling the police weed since there was so much of it to get rid of. He was supplied to the fullest with some of the best weed on the block he was told to stand on the corner of West 140th street in Harlem where crime and poverty was no stranger to this hood. the building were crumbling all around him and his partners as they stood there waiting and hoping to make a sell in the dead cold of winter he knew this was not his hood but with the cops having his back he didn't care. Word got around about how good his smoke was the people who bought it called it 'red alert weed" signaling static from one of the oldest dealers in this hood. The police that put him on had to know Daniel would be competition so they swore to protect him shit didn't get any better then this. Daniel stood there on the corner as a long black Cadillac cruised the block while him and one of his lieutenants stood on the corner waiting for the next pot head to walk up so they could make a sell. He knew a week had passed since he had seen the two cops he figure this was too good to be true there had to be a catch he wrecked his mind trying to piece shit together only coming up with nothing. Daniel had no idea the cops that put him on had a bet on his head and the pot they gave him to sell was just some shit that they picked up during a bust at a much larger dealers house. This was nothing to them they spent their days and night laid up in some of the most expensive property New York had to offer living the good life was something they was use too. Even though crime ran quit rapid in the streets in each and every small town and big city all across America suckers like Daniel came a dime a dozen when ever a quota had to be met shit would always be corrupt. Officer Briggs looked like he was in a daze as his black partner cruised the city streets looking for something to get into; the informants he had on the job looking for unsuspected sucker would call when ever some light shit came into view for a quick dollar to get that hit of crack or that hit of coke or the heroin addicted that needed that shot first thing in the morning before the shakes took them over.

"Look at them we got these mother fuckers trained Briggs." Officer Knot said as he cruised the block on the other side of Harlem 126th and 127th where the street bums, junkies and crack head held the building up with their bodies as the police cruiser cruised by them no one cared life as they seen it through rose colored glass made them not give a damn all they cared about at this point was were was their hit or shot for the day. Knots laughed he knew as long as people like this existed on the planet he would always have a job unless he got set up by one of his brothers in the department or shot in the line of duty and he hoped this wouldn't be by the hand of one of his white brothers on the force. Knot knew him and Briggs rolled as partners for three years now. Briggs, being the pimp in this situation turning his partner out putting him down with what he called some good shit. He taught him how to be a good thief, a drug dealer, and how to commit perjury if the need be and how to commit a robbery while wearing his uniform against drug dealers who didn't want to cooperate knowing that no drug dealer was dumb enough to turn him in. The police for fear of being thrown in jail himself. The code of silence these two gangsters's rolled by made them down by law after the facts of being sworn in by the department that trust they would do their best on the job.

"I was just thinking, we haven't seen our boy in two weeks let surprise him I just know he better have all the money or the drugs because if he doesn't there is no telling what I'll do to him." Briggs announced as he slid down in his seat looking at all the down trodden on the side walks of Spanish Harlem. He seen young girls as young as twelve pushing baby strollers down the sidewalks to the sight of old homeless men and woman who had been cast out on the sidewalks spending years on the street without getting any real help that could help them piece their lives back together again he knew society turned the other cheek when it came to these kinds of people, society had been faking the funk of helping the homeless all the while these people still lived on the streets, he loved the fact that young girls were having babies co-created more criminal in his eyes all blacks where potential law breakers thinking society owed them something his twisted and distorted views of society is what lead officer Briggs the crook cop he was. He co- created fear in the hood with his lily white face knowing people had labeled him as being a gung-ho slinging cop each and every time a young black male seen him roll up on them while standing on the corners trying to make a dollar off the drugs they received from officer Briggs. He thought back to his house and all the plagues and badges of honor that hung on his office wall including the one that read officer of the year of the street crimes unit this gave him a sense of power boosting up his ego preparing to make another drug arrest. Officer Briggs lived in a totally different world from that of the citizens he protected on the regular. He felt that since he risked his life on the daily for people he didn't even know this gave him the permission he needed to act out of line and become the bad cop he projected himself to be. The cruiser turned the corner putting on its cherry top as if it was going to a crime scene when there wasn't a call. He parked down the block from where Daniel was told to slinging his drugs. He was spotted Officer Briggs pulled out his top of the line binoculars to case the scene from a distance. He noticed Daniels style of dress was totally different from the way he dresses just a week ago as if he had hit the lottery.

"Look at this fool." Officer Knot said as he giggled and stuffed a jelly donut in it.

"Standing on the corner wearing a fucking Rolex watch maybe we should roll up on him right now how about it that would be the last quota for the day." Knots said looking at his partner Briggs waiting for the go ahead.

Briggs laughed to himself for he knew once he rolled up on Daniel his life on the streets would be over he would be handed a heavy sentence for the drugs he was told to sell by the cops that harassed him from selling his dresses in the streets.

"I say we give him a run for his money." Briggs announced as he put the binoculars back in there rightful place. He stepped on the gas as soon as he did the car rolled down the

Block like a bat out of hell. Daniel and his boys ran as fast as they could him not knowing who was behind the wheel held his pants up with one hand dropping any dope he had in his pockets in a long trail along the way.

"I bet you ten to one he got a gun." Briggs said as his car came to a screeching halt in front of Daniel. Daniels eyes open as wide as they could as the car almost hit him when he seen it was the two cops that put him on he smiled. Officer Briggs and officer Knot got out of their vehicle walking over to him without a smile in sight.

"So I see you got the block on lock." Officer Knots said trying to sound cool like one of Daniels boys.

"I'm doing what you ask me too. Do you have any objections about the way I'm running shit?' Daniel asks as the two big cops moved in a little closer.

"All I want to know is where is the weed and where is the money?' Briggs asks knowing Daniel had spent some without him giving him his cut.

"I didn't know you made enough money to pay for a Rolex especially from stealing dresses off the back of a truck.' Briggs said as Daniel laughed taking it as a joke.

"Listen up man you told me to sell the weed I'm selling the weed so what is the problem why all the muscle all of a sudden?' Daniel asks.

"And listen to him he's getting an attitude since we put him on you really think you're a big shot now huh?" Knots ask.

"Get in the car." Briggs said as him and his partner spun off.

"What the fuck is going on man!" Daniel yelled. The two police had taken their harassment to a whole other level making Daniel wet his pants in the fear of getting locked up.

A James Hickman Book

<u>Order this & other Bent Publishing titles</u>

_____**Do You Really Know Your Man, $15**

_____**Out Of The Game, $15**

_____**Official Contact Pages for Self Publishing, $14.95**

_____**Official Contact Pages to the Music Industry, $19.95**

_____**Official Contact Pages to the Music Industry (Dictionary), $19.95**

_____**When A Woman's Fed Up, $15 (April 2007)**

_____**Games Men Play, $15 (July 2007)**

_____**Love's Triangle, $15 (August)**

_____**Wolf In Sheep's Clothing, $15 (Sept. 2007)**

_____**Between Two Sisters, $15 (October, 2007)**

Also Available at bookstores everywhere.

<u>Use this coupon to order via mail</u>

Name_____

Address_____

City_____State_____

Zip Code_____

Shipping and Handling $5
Please allow 2-3 weeks for delivery.
    This offer subject to change without notice

Send checks or money orders to:

Bullet Entertainment Group
5441 Riverdale Rd. Suite 129
College Park, Ga 30349
www.Bentpublishing.com
Email: bulletent4000@yahoo.com

To order additional copies wholesale, please contact James Hickman at 404-246-6496 or bulletent4000@yahoo.com